Mona B. Bickerstaffe

Araki the Daimio

A Japanese Story of the Olden Time

Mona B. Bickerstaffe

Araki the Daimio
A Japanese Story of the Olden Time

ISBN/EAN: 9783337231101

Printed in Europe, USA, Canada, Australia, Japan

Cover: Foto ©Andreas Hilbeck / pixelio.de

More available books at **www.hansebooks.com**

ARAKI THE DAIMIO.

A Japanese Story of the Olden Time.

BY

MONA B. BICKERSTAFFE.

LONDON:

JACKSON, WALFORD, AND HODDER,

27, PATERNOSTER ROW.

———

1865.

CONTENTS.

—o—

viii   *Contents.*

ARAKI THE DAIMIO.

———◆———

Introduction.

It was about the middle of the sixteenth century
—an era fraught with events of weighty interest to
the Christian world in general, but more especially
to Christian England, that favoured country having
after a hard struggle succeeded in snapping the last
remaining link that bound her to the Papal chair.
How the occupant of that chair must have sighed,
sighed heavily, when forced to resign so fair a possession! and how his pontifical heart must have warmed
with rapture when, having lost his rich heritage in

B

the West, good news were brought him by Portuguese vessels heavily laden with the produce of the balmy East! There the Romish star was in its ascendant, for the "Land of the Rising Sun," having sheltered a band of shipwrecked mariners, was by them now won over to give admittance to the religion of which they were members. By-and-bye the news spread abroad, other European vessels found their way into the ports of Japan, laden not only with European merchandise, but with men zealous for the faith they professed, which, though a tainted form of Christianity, was still the religion of Christ, bearing before it the emblem of His cross. What a grand field of labour had those early Christian fathers! Then no system of exclusion existed to thwart their missionary efforts, they were free to travel through the length and breadth of the land, even as the Japanese themselves were then free to visit other countries, and mingle with foreign nations.

Truly, even the most prejudiced will allow that some of those ancient Padres were good men and true, men zealous for the glory of God, and willing to spend and be spent in His service; and of such was the successor of Francis Xavier, who himself founded fifty churches, and with his own hand baptized thirty thousand converts. But *all* were not like him; they did not *all* labour for the cause of God, and the souls of men; but some among them selfishly seeking their own advancement, grasping at everything likely to ensure temporal, as well as spiritual power, encroached *too far*, and finally lost *all*.

Rich diet did not agree with Japanese Rome any better than it did with Rome in England; when she became prosperous, she "waxed fat and kicked," and as the pride and avarice of her representative led to her overthrow in this country, in Japan, her priests finding themselves highly favoured, became arrogant and presumptuous, and not content with the many privileges they enjoyed, sought to acquire a spiritual ascendancy over the government of the land; such a bold attempt was fiercely resented by the Mikado* and the court of the Tycoon,† who, accustomed to rule with undisputed sway, could ill brook the slightest interference with their absolute and independent authority. So the seeds of distrust once sown were soon widely disseminated, fanatic fury

* Spiritual sovereign, or hereditary pontiff of Japan.
† Temporal sovereign, also called the Kubo or Djogoun.

ensued, monasteries were demolished, churches dese-
crated, and the cross of Christ (fallen into disrepute
by the evil conduct of its upholders) was torn from
its place, and trodden under foot of men.

All Christians were banished the country, the
Japanese themselves forbidden to travel, or hold any
intercourse with foreigners, the very form of their
ships being altered (by government order) so as to
prevent the possibility of their going to any distance
from their own shore. The ports of Japan were
again closed to strangers, all commerce was de-
stroyed, and the people thus shut up in their island
home, and hemmed in by a barrier of sea liable
to the most furious hurricanes, Christianity was in
time forgotten, and the Japanese dominions again
relapsed into all the horrors of heathen darkness.
So this rich and beautiful country became for a
period of two centuries as a dead letter to the rest
of the world, and her people, quiet and industrious
as they appear to be, have been until very late
years comparatively unknown to their fellow-men of
other nations.

A jealous government even now watches the movements of every foreigner who sets his foot on Japa-

nese shores; and we can scarcely wonder, when we read the history of the past, both in a religious and commercial point of view, that the Japanese should be slow to put their trust in Europeans, when the annals of their country tell so much of the dishonesty, rapacity, and insatiable cupidity of the Spanish, Portuguese, aye, and the Dutch merchants who visited their land in the sixteenth and seventeenth centuries.

It is now *our* privilege to find footing on Japanese soil, again the emblem of the cross (as borne on England's banner) is received with favour by the government, and we can only hope that in our commercial dealings with the " Land of the Rising Sun " the "greed of gain " may not be paramount, and the cause of religion forgotten, but, inasmuch as *our* faith is the *purest* form of Christianity, so those who profess it may by the purity of their lives and conduct, and the gentleness and honesty of their dealings, again win over the Japanese to *trust* the stranger, and *believe* in the stranger's God.

This is indeed our sincere desire, though we can scarcely feel sanguine as to its speedy fulfilment, for, alas! every fresh account from that " Island Empire" tells us of deep and unmitigated hostility to the foreigner, a hostility that has lately vented itself in deeds of treachery stained with blood. Yet we hope, even against hope, that all may yet be arranged without involving the destruction of hundreds of innocent beings; but in any case British diplomacy will be sorely tried in dealing with the ruling powers of Japan, who, while they are ready to resent arrogance on the part of foreigners, are equally impervious to gentle persuasion: they are not honest or truthful themselves, and early recollections do not teach them to put much faith in the honesty of Europeans. As yet we cannot trust them, nor trust our countrymen unprotected in their dominions, where a strong armed force seems necessary, if not to punish, at least to inspire respect; for, as the "Loo Choo" native said, "Japan man very cunning; if he see you strong, he very civil, suppose you too civil he take your head."* So we must not be too civil, nor yet too severe, but if by our firmness and consistency we succeed in teaching them to respect our banner, we may by and bye induce them to listen to the story of its emblem. But we have digressed from the thread of our tale, which is not of the present, but of the olden time.

* See "Beecher's Voyage of the Samarang."

CHAPTER I.

———

Night wanes—the vapours round the mountains curled
Melt into morn, and Light awakes the world—
Man has another day to swell the past,
And lead him near to little but his last;
But mighty nature bounds as from her birth,
The sun is in the heavens, and life on earth;
Flowers in the valley, splendour in the beam,
Health on the gale, and freshness in the stream.

BYRON.

IT was early morning : a glorious sunrise had dispelled the darkness of a stormy night, and the Lake of Hakoni which a few hours before had resembled a dark and boiling cauldron, now lay like a sheet of silver calmly reflecting a sky of the clearest blue. The steep hills rising abruptly from the water cast dark shadows below, while their green slopes were tinted to a rosy hue, and behind them the conical

peak of Fusi-yama* the Matchless, towered high
above the clouds, from whence its snow-capped
summit peeped forth, all in a glory, bright as of
burnished gold.

Pausing for a moment to paint the picture that
morning presented to the view, we must fancy ourselves on the high ground immediately above the
Lake, from whence the scene is truly rich and varied.
Broad plains stretching away to the sea, which, even
at this early hour, is specked with numberless fish-
ing-boats, while farther off the white sails of outward
bound trading-junks glitter in the sunshine and break
the outline of the blue horizon. Pretty little hamlets
dotting the banks of winding streams, and surrounded
by grassy fields and rich crops waving for the harvest,
give evidence of an industrious and thriving population, while the dark outlines of primeval forests of
pine and cedar, oak, and spreading beech, present
every hue of luxuriant foliage. Descending from
our post of observation, we are fain to linger a
moment more to admire that grove of stately pines,
alas! sadly thinned by the storm of last night, for

---

* Fusi-yama the Matchless, or, the Holy Mountain, is held in
great reverence by the people of Japan.

here and there great branches are strewn about, and more than one giant of the forest torn from its roots lies stretched across the road. It is not a road in the common acceptation of the word, but rather an avenue leading to the residence of a wealthy Daimio,* and men are busy in all directions clearing off the fallen timber, and making the way passable. We wonder why they are in such desperate haste, and we shall wonder still more if we enter the place, for there is some unwonted cause breaking the calm monotony that usually reigns supreme. This morning every one is alive and active, for Araki the Daimio, and richest landowner in the neighbourhood of Hakoni, is about to set out on his periodical visit to Yeddo,† and such a man of quality cannot undertake such a journey without causing considerable bustle at his departure.

Few of the Daimios enjoy this long journey and forced residence at the capital; but Araki is not one of those who are content with a quiet life of luxurious

---

* Daimio, a Japanese lord.

† Capital of the Tycoons; the Daimios are compelled to pass six months in the year at Yeddo, and during their absence at their country mansions, their wives, children, and many of their servants remain as hostages for their good behaviour.

ease, he is a proud, ambitious man, a Daimio by hereditary right; a staunch Tory (as it were), indignant
at the introduction of new people, novel customs, and
still more at the progress of the new religion that is
spreading itself through the landof his fathers. Indeed,
the great lord contemplates his ourney to Yeddo with
peculiar satisfaction; for it gives him an opportunity
of using his influence at court for the suppression
of Christianity, and the expulsion of Christians. But
h e will have to act with much guile and secrecy,
for at present it would not be good policy to show
open hostility, seeing that many of his brother
Daimios have embraced the new religion; it has
spread itself into the army, and even the Emperor,
the great Fide Yosé, or Taikosama, regards it with
such favour that but for his harem delights, which
he cannot, and will not relinquish, he would become
a member of the new faith.

These thoughts are uppermost in the mind of
Araki, as he enjoys his morning meal, while a richly
painted norimon* stands at the principal entrance to
his mansion, round which an immense concourse of retainers are collected, waiting the appearance of their

* A sort of sedan used by the Japanese in travelling.

lord. There are the patient half-naked coolies, list-lessly smoking their little pipes, but ready at a moment's notice to bear the norimon aloft on their brawny shoulders ; there are grooms holding richly caparisoned horses, servants with the armorial bear-ings of their lord embroidered on the backs and shoulders of their clothes, archers and matchlock men, Yakomins* and officers with two swords, and others of inferior grade, who are only entitled to wear one. These are all whiling away the time in their own peculiar fashion ; some refreshing themselves with tea and saki, some indulging in serious conversation, and others resting on their heels, and silently enjoy-ing the weed.

The place they are in is a sort of court-yard, but, instead of being surrounded by walls, it is bounded by trees and shrubs, some growing in natural beauty, and others dwarfed into quaint forms of cows and monkeys, men and demons. Through these trees may be seen sheltered alcoves, leading to lovely gar-dens, from whence you even now hear the cooing of doves, and the less musical voices of the gaily painted parrot and peacock. Presently there is a

* Yakomins, or Samourai, Japanese police.

hushing, hissing sound; a Yakomin waves his fan, and all present make a low reverence, their foreheads touching the ground, and their bodies almost concealed by the attitude of their heads and knees. We look for the cause of this sudden movement, and see a tall dark man standing at the door of the house. His figure is portly; the features of his face are well-formed, and but for a certain prominence in the cheek-bones, we can detect no sign of Tartar origin; his countenance, when smiling, has a pleasant expression, but there is dark fire in his sinister eyes that speaks of slumbering volcanoes, and makes us feel that we would rather not excite his anger or malice. He is dressed in a simple traveling costume; wide loose trowsers, a skirt of fine grass-cloth, striped blue and white, with a tunic of the same pattern, but a thicker material; this is confined at the waist by a broad silken sash, in which two swords are inserted. These weapons appear to be of very fine workmanship—one much longer than the other—having a hilt almost as long as its blade. This hilt is marked with many devices, indicative of the great rank of the wearer; on the outer side we see his armorial bearings richly

wrought in gold, and covered with a delicate net-
work, which protects, without concealing its beauty.
A cup-shaped guard is attached, more for ornament
than use, and this is also decorated with a knob
of pure gold.

The second sword is similar, but has a shorter hilt,
it is enclosed in a scabbard of shagreen, and is
never drawn but in extreme cases, and then can only
be resheathed when it has shed blood. So much for
the appearance of Araki the Daimio, who, stepping
into his norimon, is soon doubled up in what we
should consider a position of questionable comfort,
while he is borne along, smoking in silent dignity,
his body inactive, but his deep mind revolving all
the plots and intrigues which he purposes to carry
out during his six months' residence at the capital.

Let us follow his procession for a little way, and
watch it as it enters yonder dark defile. There are
first the runners, whose business it is to give warning
of the great man's approach; then the two standard-
bearers, the tops of their spears decorated with the
tuft of black feathers distinctive of the presence of a
Daimio; next come a company of officers and personal attendants, then grooms with led horses, more

servants, the norimon containing the Daimio, a group
of inferior officers, extra norimon-bearers, baggage and
baggage-porters, umbrella-bearers, again more servants,
Yakomins, and officers; and so the cortège ends, and
we leave it for awhile, to pursue its journey to Yeddo,
over roads of the most primitive description, rough
and rutty, and in many places ploughed into deep
furrows by last night's torrents of rain, real "corduroy
roads," over which it would be impossible to ride or
drive without imminent danger to man and beast,
but through whose deep trenches the coolies wade
with the utmost unconcern, keeping the line in a slow
jog-trot, quite content in the knowledge that they
need not add to their fatigues by undue haste, for
if they plod on steadily they must in time reach some
halting place where they may rest awhile and recruit
their exhausted energies by a few refreshing whiffs
from their ever-beloved pipes.

CHAPTER II.

———

. . . . The forms of life
Impress their characters on the smooth forehead ;
Nought sinks into the bosom's silent depth.
Quick sensibility of pain and pleasure
Moves the light fluids lightly ; but *no* soul
Warmeth the inner frame.

SCHILLER.

WE left the Daimio of Hakoni pursuing his journey
to Yeddo, and perhaps it may be interesting to some
of my readers, if we follow him on his route, as he
travels, from "morn till dewy eve," at a rate that
is never allowed to exceed twenty miles per day.
We are prone to envy him, borne along in luxurious
ease, every comfort provided, and untroubled by a
single care ; but we cannot envy, we rather pity, one

who feels no pleasure in the beauty of each varied scene, who knows not how to esteem the works of nature, or to recognise in them the presence of nature's God. Yet what a rich and beautiful country is that through which he passes! See those open plains where paddy (or rice) fields, of exquisite green, form a bright contrast to the golden hue of the ripe and waving corn. There are broad hedges of the tea-plant, and its sister, the fair camellia; here the pomegranate, the nectarine, the almond, the peach, and the fragrant orange, delight us, by the rich beauty of their varied hues, while the honey-suckle and the "wilding rose" trail lovingly among the branches of their more gorgeous confrères. So much floral beauty would almost weary us, if the eye were not occasionally relieved by the tall branches of the light bamboo and the shining leaves of the evergreen oak. Even the latter is sometimes made gay, against its will, when the beautiful wisteria creeps among its boughs, and enlivens its dark branches with laughing clusters of pendent blossom. But all is not beauty on the road to Yeddo; there are dreary mud flats to be crossed, on broad ladders, that shake unpleasantly when they are trodden by the horses and the heavily-laden coolies; and we wonder whether the dignity of the Daimio can ever be disturbed, and whether he feels the least bit uneasy, as the yielding soil seems threatening to open and swallow him in its swampy depths. Perhaps he has not noticed the change of scene, for there he sits smoking, with his usual apathy, though I am sure his norimon must have had many an uncomfortable shake, both here and in yonder rushing stream, over which it has been borne aloft by the ever-submissive coolies.

Ere night comes on, the travellers reach a small town, noisy enough before their appearance; but the vendors of cooked fish and sweetmeats soon make themselves scarce, having no desire to encounter the insolence and cruelty of the Daimio's two-sworded retainers. Arriving at this town, the party halt before a spacious-looking building. It is the Honjen,* or Inn, whose proprietors are bound to receive the Daimios with their suites, and any other officers of the Tycoon whose business or pleasure takes them that way.

Here Araki condescends to alight, and is received

---

* The Honjens, or public inns (like everything else in Japan), are under Government surveillance.

at the entrance by the host; but we cannot see whether the countenance of the latter, ruddy and beaming, gives promise of good cheer, for mine host of the Honjen of Sin'syu receives his illustrious visitors with his forehead touching the ground, and remains in that apoplectic attitude until Araki has passed into the house; nor does he again venture to intrude himself into his presence, until, with equal humility, he has the pleasure of seeing him off again the following morning.

Albeit the great empty-looking Honjen has no outward appearance of comfort beyond abundance of fresh air and excessive cleanliness, yet it has culinary attractions to tempt the hungry, and soft rugs, with well-padded counterpanes, to rest the weary limbs; and we confess the great Araki looks like a very ordinary mortal as he lies on the matted floor, tightly tucked up, his head reposing on no downy pillow, but on a kind of convex padded rest. Yet we must suppose that his slumbers have been refreshing, for by daybreak he is up again, and ready for the road. Again the party muster in the courtyard, and sweep out of the town with no small amount of bustle and confusion; and it is well if the inhabitants of the peaceful hamlet have no cause to regret their brief residence among them.

A little way out of Sin'syu, they meet another party, less pretentious, but quite as large as their own. They are pilgrims on their way to the Holy Mountain; and, having rested during the night at that little temple just peeping from yonder dark grove of firs, the Bonzes* are fain to escort them a little way on the road. But now the Bonzes turn back, bearing, with proud step, their sacred emblems and banners; while the poor pilgrims travelling on their way advance towards the Daimio party. The road is narrow, and we wonder how they will all pass; but a voice cries, "Shitanirio!"† A fan is waved; the pilgrims fall on their faces; and the great lord sweeps on between walls of doubled-up humanity.

So the journey goes on from day to day, with no incident of note to disturb its serenity. The Honjens are all the same; and where there are no Honjens, the travellers halt at roadside places of rest, where, if they have nothing else, plenty of ripe fruit and fresh fish can be had for a mere trifle

---

* Native priests.
† Shitanirio,—kneel down.

Now and then, they meet a party of peasants on their way to market, or returning from their day's labour; a group of fishermen, with their broad basket-hats and picturesque costume, not unlike that of our northern Celts; a troop of jolly beggars; or a party of itinerant musicians on their way to the nearest town. It is well for these poor creatures if they see the Daimio's retinue in time to get out of their way, otherwise they will be very likely to suffer; for, as the great lord passes by in state, he does not trouble himself as to the conduct of his followers; he heeds not the agony of the yelping cur as it writhes under the pain of a passing sword-cut, or the cries of grief when some poor peasant has fallen in the same manner.

What cares he for life or death? Even his own existence is of little value to him; and he would shorten it at any moment rather than suffer the slightest disgrace. The dog's death and the peasant's are the same in his eyes; for the Daimio, although wise in all the learning of his ancient nation, is but a poor ignorant heathen: he knows of no heaven, and fears no hell.

But he is destined to suffer for the misconduct of

his followers, of which he is guilty, inasmuch as he allows it to go unpunished.

They had been enjoying refreshment at a tea-house, where some of the party must have inhaled something much stronger than tea, even potent saki ;* for, as they left the place, more than one of the two-sworded officers were in an advanced stage of intoxication, in which condition it was their pleasure to attack everything that came in their way; and even those who, peaceably inclined, tried to avoid an encounter with such dangerous fellows. They lingered behind the rest of the party, the better to carry out their mischievous pranks; but for a long while the road was lonely, and they had no opportunity of displaying their tipsy valour. At length they spy a number of people coming their way, dressed in sombre garments, their heads completely enveloped in deep basket-work hats, that fell like extinguishers over their faces. These they knew to be penitents,† and, therefore, fair game for roystering fellows like themselves. Their lord's norimon was so far in advance

---

* Intoxicating spirit used by the Japanese.

† Penitents are generally disgraced officers; they have no means of support, but wander about begging.

as to be almost out of sight, so they threw themselves
in the way of the penitents, attacked them with
insulting language, and tried to pull off their hats;
but the latter were not going to be insulted with
impunity: they made a stout resistance, and tried to
defend themselves with their staves. A regular row
ensued. The officers slashed about them with their
naked swords, inflicting fearful wounds; many of the
penitents were killed, and the rest fled, uttering vows
of deadly vengeance, which only excited the mirth of
their drunken assailants. But too soon these had
reason to repent of their swaggering; for, as the
evening drew on, and the party were slowly toiling
down a steep mountain path (or rather the dry bed
of a mountain torrent), overhung by rocks and clusters of fir-trees, they were astonished by a sudden
shower of stones and arrows. The Daimio's attendants placed themselves in an attitude of defence, and
returned the attack by a volley into the nearest
thicket, which must have done considerable execution, for it was followed by a scream of rage, and
soon after the assailants rushed from their ambush,
causing the air to ring with their frightful yells,
and singling out those who had mingled in the affray

of the morning, they killed them on the spot, and
rushed back to their hiding-place before the others
could recover their surprise. Then it was that the
Daimio's party understood the mistake they had made,
for the apparently harmless penitents who had been
wantonly murdered by them were really Lonins* (or
robbers), who had assumed that defenceless disguise
the better to elude public justice when crossing the
open country. Those who escaped had contrived to
reach the haunts of their comrades in time to warn
them of the approach of the travellers, thus speedily
fulfilling their vows of vengeance; which done, they
appeared no more to molest them.

Their enemies gone, the travellers pursue their
journey, but they are in a sadly crippled state, for, as
is often the case, the innocent have suffered with the
guilty: one of the horses lies dead, and many of the
poor coolies have been so sorely wounded that they
drop down and die by the way, and to crown their
misfortunes an arrow has found its way into the
norimon, and is lodged in the portly person of its

---

* It is a common practice of the Lonins to assume the dress of
penitents, which being a complete disguise enables them to pass
through the country unobserved.

occupant. With admirable self-possession Araki draws the weapon from the wound, and gives orders to his attendants to proceed with the utmost dispatch in the direction of yonder park-like grounds, which are just seen in the distance, and which enclose the residence of a gentleman with whom he is sure to find a hospitable welcome, and the sheltering rest which in his present wounded state he very sorely needs. With Araki's servants, to hear is to obey; and very soon they reach the gates leading to the house, where the state of the case is no sooner known than the owner of the mansion appears, and with many salaams and softly uttered words of welcome assists the Daimio from his norimon, and leads him into the house, in which his principal officers also find quarters, while the humbler sort are provided for in the neighbouring hamlet. His wound has robbed Araki of his usual lofty bearing: he walks with uncertain steps, for he is weak from pain and exhaustion, and he very gladly allows himself to be laid on a soft mat, where he soon faints from loss of blood. And there we leave him to be carefully tended by an old Isi-ya (or doctor), while we wander over the mansion of Sako Miyako, and take a glance at its internal arrangements. It is a light and elegant structure, consisting of numerous apartments, separated from each other by thin partitions, which being moveable the whole of one floor may at any time be converted into one large room. These apartments are divided into two suites, those on one side being appropriated to the females of the family (and into these strangers are never allowed to intrude), all general visitors being received in the other rooms, which answer to our reception or drawing-rooms. In these we see large vases of a coarse description of porcelain, usually filled with tea; paintings, manuscripts, curious books, arms, and armorial bearings. They are bare of furniture, but the floors are covered with thick rugs or mats, bordered with a rich fringe, which mats (according to an ancient custom or government order) are each of them six feet long and three feet wide. The walls are hung with embroidery, or pithy sentences, proverbs and moral maxims, emblazoned in letters of gold and colours. The doors are covered with paper, on which is traced the most elegant designs of fruit and flowers in gold and silver, while the ceilings are embellished with beautiful paintings. The windows, low and open, are

filled with vases of flowers; singing birds flit about in
cages of the most delicate workmanship: indeed, birds
and flowers are everywhere, giving the house a de-
lightfully cheerful aspect.

It is just the place for an invalid to like to lie
still and dream away his days, allowing Nature quietly
to work her own cure.

But Araki, though keenly alive to sensual enjoyment, is not the man to be quietly happy in this
charming retreat; for though his body is at rest,
his mind is ill at ease, his thoughts are not thoughts
of peace, and his spirit chafes within him as he longs
to push on to the capital, and plunge into the political
vortex ere the tide of events becomes too strong for
him to stem against it.

CHAPTER III.

———

IT is evening: many days have passed since Araki
the Daimio was brought in wounded to the residence
of Sako Miyako ; during the interval he has gone
through an attack of fever, against which his
powerful constitution has had some trouble in fighting its way. But he is now convalescent, and
again able to enjoy his favourite pipe ; and we see
him thus employed as he reposes on the mat close
by an open window, through which the evening

breeze steals softly, bearing on its pinions delicious odours, and sweetest notes of feathered songsters. But, hark! there is melody of another nature, and Araki actually takes the pipe from his mouth while he listens entranced to strains that he has never heard before: even the very language is unknown to him; and ere he has had time to recover from his sensations of surprise and pleasure, the notes have died away, and the soft cooing of the ring-dove is the only sound he hears. Araki rises and steps into the garden, which at one side is skirted by a shady lane: down this lane the choristers have passed, for it leads to an unpretending little edifice, with neither tower nor minaret, only a simple cross to tell what it is. The doors are open, and as Araki passes at that side of the garden again, the sweet music falls on his ear. Sweet and solemn, soft and thrilling, are the notes of that Portuguese evening hymn, and the Daimio listens eagerly while the music lasts; but when it ceases, its benign influence passes away, and, like Saul of old, the evil spirit again takes possession of him, and he stamps with fury, as his proud heathen nature rebels against the innovations of strangers and the strangers' creed into the

"Land of the Rising Sun." But his rage does not, to outward appearance, last very long: he soon betakes himself again to his favourite weed, and, soothed by it, he wanders about in his usual calm, abstracted manner. Presently he is joined by his host, and the two salaam and compliment each other, and converse after their fashion in low tones in their soft and flowery language. We know not what subject they have chosen : perhaps Sako Miyako is doing the honours of his demesne, and pointing out its various beauties to his great court friend; and we can pardon him if he is proud of the paradise he calls his own, with its green lawns and bits of wilderness, where gold and silver pheasants wander at will, its fish-ponds alive with water-fowl, among which we notice the gorgeous mandarin drake floating by the side of his plain-looking partner, while the solemn stork stands looking into the water, apparently indulging in grave meditations, but really intently watching his prey. Here artificial rockwork rises from banks gay with the Chinese pink and Japanese day-lily, while cascades glitter in the sunshine, as they tumble over real rocks into reservoirs full of gold and silver fish.

The gardens extend all round the house, and a person walking in these can see through the open windows into the broad apartments; and Araki, apathetic as he is, should be more than mortal if he could pass by one particular window without pausing a moment to contemplate the pretty scene within; nor does Sako prevent him from doing so, for the old man feels a father's pride in that particular portion of his property. Let us follow the direction of Araki's eyes into a room void of furniture, but decorated with costly ornaments,— vases of the most delicate porcelain, cabinets of inlaid ivory and lacquer work, vessels of rare beauty filled with the choicest cosmetics and perfumes, carvings of exquisite workmanship, jewelled ornaments for the toilet; in fact, everything the most costly, rare, and beautiful that Japanese art can produce. But amid all this collection of treasure there is one object that particularly attracts the Daimio. It is a fair young girl, slender in form, and below the middle height, with full grey eyes, and a well-shaped head adorned with a profusion of glossy dark hair, that is becomingly drawn back and fastened behind in a graceful top-knot. She is seated on the ground in her native fashion, her hands resting on her knees, and the loose wide sleeves of her richly embroidered jacket partially revealing her delicately moulded arms. Her flowing robe is confined at the waist by a broad silken sash, while one tiny foot peeps forth unfettered by a shoe, beside it lying a little sandal of the finest plaited rice grass.

Three pretty laughter-loving damsels lounge in graceful attitudes round her ; they are clad in garments of chequered cotton, tied at the waists with huge bows, and so scanty in the skirts that they must considerably impede their powers of locomotion. They are merry Hebe-looking beings, evidently formed for mirth and happiness ; lovers of music too, and of song, for musical instruments lie scattered about, and books of poems, with which they and their fair mistress while away the days of their life. An innocent life truly, as their knowledge lies ; yet to us not life, but rather a dream, an aimless existence, with no self-imposed duties to perform, and if it be without cares, it is equally without hope to cheer in sickness or in sorrow. Suddenly the doors open, and a train of attendants glide into the room, bearing lacquered trays on a level with their chins. These contain sweetmeats and fruit, transparent china cups full of fragrant tea, and slender pipes with tiny bowls of gold, and mouthpieces of the purest silver. These they deposit beside the ladies, and retire as noiselessly as they came.

It is thus that Ama, the only daughter of Sako Miyako, is daily waited upon: she has everything this world can give her,—a doting parent, pleasant companions, and servants ready to do her slightest bidding; and yet the fair girl is not happy, for she has lately learned that this life is not the end of human existence, but rather a period of probation, during which she must strive 'to attain to a holier and happier state of being. She has tried to interest her young companions in the subject of her meditations, but they do not respond to her feelings : they are too volatile to trouble themselves about the future, they do not wish to be disturbed in their present state of happiness; and could they speak our language, they would exclaim, "Where ignorance is bliss, 'twere folly to be wise." But Ama thinks much of these things, both with reference to herself and her aged father, whose term of

life must soon draw to a close ; and then—
what then? At the very moment that Sako
appeared at the window, she was anxiously revolving that question in her mind, thinking anxiously
of him and her dead mother, and wondering whether
those parted by death will indeed meet again—up
there ; and the young girl raised her lustrous eyes
to heaven, and longed to penctrate its blue vault
and behold the realm of angels commanded by the
Great Monarch, in whom "we also live and move
and have our being."

It was just at that moment that Araki saw the
maiden, and was struck by her wondrous beauty ;
he could not have told why he thought her more
lovely than the fair ones who adorn his harem at
Yeddo, some of whom are almost faultlessly beautiful : yet how different from Ama! Her loveliness is
of a style altogether new to him ; it does not consist
in mere feature, but in the glory of a newly
awakened intellect, and a countenance whose beauty
is enhanced by the pure light of an aspiring soul.

We are not to suppose that Araki is all this time
staring at the maiden ; such conduct would be a
sad breach of Japanese etiquette. Having seen Ama

D

once, he is resolved; so he passes on with her father and converses of other things, while she closes her reverie with a soft sigh, takes the tiny cup handed to her by one of her maidens, and turns to the calm enjoyment of their evening meal. She has scarcely seen her father's visitor, yet a shudder passes over her delicate frame as she for a moment recalls the fixed gaze of that tall, dark man.

CHAPTER IV.

"Let this barbarous Lord despair
His purposed aim to win;
Let him take living, land, and life,
But to be Marmion's wedded wife
    In me were deadly sin."
                                        SCOTT.

SAKO MIYAKO, to whose hospitality the Daimio of
Hakoni was indebted for recovery from the effects
of his wound, though a man of great wealth, did not
belong to the nobles of Japan, but held a rank equi-
valent to that of a country squire in England. He
had high interest with the government, and might
have been made a Daimio, but he preferred living in
retirement to being whirled into the vortex of court

intrigue, and being forced to leave his beautiful home each year, for a six months' residence at Yeddo. His eldest son held a high position among the officers of the Tycoon, and to him the father delegated all ambitious views for advancing the glory of his ancient race; while the second son, who was a merchant at Simoda, was certainly *not* decreasing its wealth and prosperity. His business bringing him into frequent contact with the Portuguese traders, he very soon became impregnated with their opinions; indeed, it could not be supposed that people so active in the missionary cause would have allowed him to pass in and out among them without making an effort at his conversion. Nor did they rest there; but having secured one member of a wealthy family, they hastened to extend their influence through all its branches. Sako Yoriama was of a soft, plastic disposition,— one who, never daring to have an opinion of his own, was the more easily led by stronger minds; in fact, though a keen man in worldly affairs, he was in things spiritual just the being to become a willing convert and unquestioning disciple of the Church of Rome. Yoriama could not rest until he had imparted his new views to his relatives; nor was it the desire

of his instructors that he should remain quiescent:
therefore, on proselyting thoughts intent, combined
with mercantile transactions to be executed by the
way, the Christian merchant set out for his father's
home, and during his brief residence there contrived to win over his gentle sister to listen to the
Gospel tidings, and to read those historical parts
of Holy Writ which the learned priests had, with
much labour, translated into the Japanese language.
Ama's mind was differently constituted to her brother's
—it was of a higher order, and, instead of becoming
fettered, it expanded under her newly acquired knowledge. The history of the Creation filled her with
wonder, and led her to regard every object in nature
with a newly-awakened interest. The fall of our first
parents saddened her; she felt angry at their dis-
obedience, that brought sin and sorrow into a sinless
Paradise: yet she pitied them, when she thought
how she should feel if driven forth from her home,
to wander in a dreary waste. But most of all were
the young girl's sympathies awakened by the story
of the Cross; while her tender heart beat with loving
gratitude to Him who died that she might live. The
brother did not rest with exciting his sister's interest

only, but used all his influence with his father to win him also to the Christian faith; but Sako, loving his heathen gods, would not relinquish them at once, though he made no objection to a Christian church being erected on his property, even close by his own residence.

The Padre whose mission it was to officiate at this little church, was a man who had chosen the sacred office, and finally the missionary life, from feelings of real piety. He had passed through the most overwhelming sorrow; his younger days had not been unstained by crime, but now he only lived to grieve over the past, and to thank God for the afflictions that had led him to repentance. His manners were gentle and winning; his bearing humble and subdued, for he never forgot what he had been; and the remembrance of the past filled him with sad humility. This good man took a real fatherly interest in Ama; it grieved him to see one so lovely wasting away the most precious hours of life, and he used every effort to win her confidence, and induce her to read the books which he was only too happy to lend her. The strictly secluded life which etiquette entails on Japanese ladies was a great barrier to his efforts; but the Padre

was patient, and watched his opportunities; and though
he could not visit the maiden at her house, he often
spoke to her as he passed down the lane, and learned
with pleasure that she lingered in the gardens, and
listened with intense delight to the music of the
morning and vesper services. Lately he had been
talking to her on the subject of Baptism, but Ama
hesitated before taking the final step; for she doubted
whether her father would ever give his consent to
her openly renouncing the faith of their fatherland.
Thus it was that Ama was for a long while a Christian
in heart, before she dared openly to profess herself a
follower of Christ; and it was while she was in this
waiting, pupa stage of her spiritual existence, that
the Daïmio of Hakoni visited at her paternal house.
We may, therefore, imagine the feelings she experienced, when, before his departure, she received,
through her father, the proud lord's proposal to
become his wife. In a worldly point of view, the
alliance was a splendid one; and perhaps some time
ago Ama would not have strenuously objected to
be the favourite wife of such a great man: but
now all her ideas were changed. She could not
now be content to share a harem with half-a-dozen

other wives, and she recoiled with horror from a fate that would deprive her of all freedom of thought and will, and place her in a position nothing better than affluent slavery. No, she could not be the Daimio's bride; for was he not a bigoted heathen, fiercely hating the Christian and the Christian faith? In vain old Sako argued and reasoned, laying before her the advantages of Araki's offer. Ama would not listen to it for a moment; and as the old man heard her entreating him not to force her to leave him in his solitary old age, his heart was drawn toward her, and he began to think that his beautiful home would indeed be dreary, if robbed of the calm light of her gentle presence.

Araki was inflamed with rage and disappointment at Ama's very decided rejection of his suit. It was something new to him to be refused anything on which he had set his heart, and to be thwarted in his dearest hopes by a mere child was especially galling to his pride.

Had Sako himself any objection to the marriage? No: Sako was only too proud that the great Sama*

---

* Sama,—lord.

should confer so high a compliment on his very humble servant.

Then why should not an obstinate girl be compelled to obey?

But at this the old man (albeit with many salaams and expressions of high-flown compliment) gave signs of dissent. He had lately found new beauties in his daughter: new love for her had sprung up to warm his aged heart; and he was not now the man to compel her to anything that would cause her such misery as she had assured him would certainly follow her marriage with Araki. So the Daimio left the mansion of his friend with anything but friendly feelings to its inmates; and though he entered his norimon with many genuflexions and courtly expressions of gratitude, the dark light in his eye belied the soft "saionara"* on his lips, for it spoke a language that seemed to say—"Farewell; but you'll hear from me again."

Perhaps, if he had been able to pass directly to the stirring scenes of court life, his feelings might have proved as effervescent as they had been sudden; but

* Saionara—the Japanese adieu.

shut up in his norimon, with no other company than his own thoughts, even courtly intrigues were forgotten in the tumult of conflicting passions that made him their prey, and the only satisfaction he derived during the rest of his journey was in venting his rage on those about him ; a common source of comfort for the unenlightened pagan, and one too often followed by those who, in *name* at least, are educated Christians.

CHAPTER V.

———

" These are Thy glorious works, Parent of good,
  Almighty! Thine this universal frame,
  Thus wondrous fair: Thyself how wondrous then,
  Unspeakable! who sitt'st above these heavens
  To us invisible, or dimly seen
  In these Thy lowest works; yet these declare
  Thy goodness beyond thought, and power divine."
                  MILTON.

SAKO MIYAKO, though always courteous to the Christian missionary, for a long while refused to listen to his teaching, until at length accident (or, rather, Providence) opened a way for the good man's words to reach those ears that were "dull of hearing."

The day had been fine, but dark and sultry, the atmosphere unusually heavy; an oppressive stillness reigned everywhere, and it seemed as if nature was

standing still, in waiting expectation of some great
event. Suddenly the air is slightly stirred, a hissing
wind agitates the light bamboos and sobs through
the branches of the tallest pines; the birds and beasts
move about uneasily, and a feeling of fear seems to
pervade all animated creation. The household of
Sako are pursuing their various avocations, when the
ground begins to vibrate under their feet, gently at
first, so as to be barely perceptible, but gradually
with an increase of motion that by and by assumes
a fearful violence. The house sways to and fro;
everything moveable is hurled from its place; the
beams and woodwork groan as if about to be wrenched
asunder by some giant force; and the inmates, fearful
of more convulsive throes, rush out into the open air,
and throw themselves on their faces to the ground.
Terror reigns everywhere; but one slight form may
be seen in the midst of the prostrate figures, with
a pale but steadfast countenance, upturned eyes, and
lips that move as if in prayer. It is Ama, who is
thus awaiting the issue of the earthquake, meanwhile seeking protection from the All-powerful Being
in whom she has lately learned to trust. Her
father and all those about her believe that the

shock has been caused by the uneasy movements of
that Great Dragon whom their heathen fancy has
placed in the centre of the earth, who vomits forth
flame from the volcanoes, and shakes the world when
he is angry. Of the scientific cause of earthquakes,
and of volcanic agency, Ama knows nothing, but she
does know that there is One God who rules heaven
and earth, and, with childlike faith and simple trust,
she relies on *Him* for protection. She had taken her
father's head in her lap while the earth was trembling,
and now that the danger is over the old man ven-
tures to look up, awe and wonder depicted in his
almost livid countenance, while he inquires why his
" moos'me" fears not the wrath of the Great Dragon.
Now, Ama is not prepared to refute the idea of the
Great Dragon's existence, (being ignorant of any
other reason to assign for the earthquake), so she
simply replies, " Because I believe in another who is
greater than he." Then she takes from the folds of
her robe a little book, and reads the story of the
beginning of time, when the earth was " without
form and void, and darkness was upon the face of
the deep;" when the Almighty voice cried, " Let
there be light! and there was light;" when at the

same voice the barren waste became clothed with
verdure, trees and flowers burst forth in their beauty,
and birds, and beasts, and creeping things sprang
into life; when a handful of dust, under the same
Almighty influence, became a perfect form, modelled
after the image, and breathing the very essence of
his Great Creator. Ama carefully read the account
of those six periods of time, during which the "Great
Architect" was busy at His work, and then she appealed
to her father's reason to know if He who made all
things should not be trusted as the best Preserver of
the work of His hands. At that moment the Padre
José appearing in the lane, he was invited into the
garden. The late dsi-sin-nai (earthquake) was of
course the subject of conversation; and the good
man was not slow in improving the opportunity, when
he perceived the hitherto dark mind of Sako Miyako
to be awakened to serious reflection. Skilfully he
went over the same ground that Ama had trod before,
showing also the folly of trusting in gods who could
not help themselves; for if the deities of Japan had
indeed power to contend with the Author of the
universe, why did they allow one of their sacred
edifices to become a pile of ruins? And taking his

hearers to a part of the garden that commanded a
distant view, he pointed to a column of smoke, from
whence issued streams of flaming fire, that marked
the funereal pile of the great temple of the god
Otango. This course of reasoning was unanswerable.
Sako henceforth lost faith in his heathen idols and
turned to the One true God ; and so it fell, that when
Ama was baptized in the Christian faith, she did not
go alone to the sacred font, for her aged father also
received the sign of the cross, and promised to fight
manfully under its banner against the world, the
devil, and the flesh. So all was henceforth doubly
peaceful in the residence of Sako Miyako, the Japanese
gentleman and his daughter living in love and Christian unity, striving to do good in their generation,
and becoming more and more attached to the Christian faith. Longing openly to show their love for
Christ, they built a school for the poor, and an
hospital for the sick, and enlarged and embellished
the little Christian church after a manner consistent
with their ideas of the beautiful; for as they had
formerly delighted to honour the Temple of Otango,
so they now felt a deeper and more reverential pride
in the house of the true God. In all this the good

Padre José was their guide and instructor, but he did not encourage any lavish expenditure or gorgeous display : he led them to benefit the poor and afflicted, but his own tastes were simple, almost ascetic, and no extra comforts or luxuries found their way into his private home from the wealth of his Japanese converts. And now we must leave him and his little flock in the calm enjoyment of holy peace, while we travel to far different scenes, and far different people, even to Yeddo, the great capital of the Tycoon.

CHAPTER VI.

———

. . . . "As the sun,
Ere it is risen, sometimes paints its image
In the atmosphere, so often do the spirits
Of great events stride on before the events,
And in to-day already walks to-morrow."

SCHILLER.

WHEN Araki the Daimio arrived at Yeddo, he
found many things to rekindle the wrath which,
ignited by his late disappointment, had somewhat
cooled down before he reached the end of his journey.
First, it was not very agreeable to his feelings, on
entering the city, to find himself immediately in the
rear of a grand religious procession,—Spaniards and
Portuguese, with their priests and laymen, wearing
their richest robes, while several of the native princes,

E

with all their officers and dependants, swelled the
brilliant throng. How the Daimio scowled as he saw
them pass on, absorbing the public attention, while
he, for once in his life, was allowed to go on his way
unheeded! What a hell of malice was stirred up in
his heart, and what fixed determination mantled on
his brow, as he entered within the gates of his own
splendid residence! The Daimio's town mansion was
of a different appearance to those country residences
which we have lately been describing. It was evidently built more with an eye to strength than
beauty, separated from the street by a deep muddy
ditch, or moat, and with a long line of barred windows, extending for an immense distance at each side
of the great entrance. These windows, seldom un-
occupied, were then filled with eager faces, looking
down with anxious interest at the arrival of their
friends from the country; for this side of the mansion was set apart to the great lord's retainers and
servants: his own more luxurious apartments, shun-
ning the vulgar gaze, opened not into the street, but
into beautiful gardens and pleasure-grounds.

It needed no very great amount of skill to stir up

the mind of Taiko Sama against the foreigners, both laymen and priests. Formerly, having viewed Christianity solely from a religious point of view, he was by no means inclined to interfere with it or its teachers; indeed, to him one form of religion seemed as good as another; and as his own contained thirty-six varieties (all thriving peaceably in his dominions), he did not see why one more or less might not be tolerated. When, therefore, Araki arrived at Yeddo, and was as usual received into the most secret councils of its ruler, the wily politician, instead of expressing open hostility to the Christians, showed himself perfectly peaceable in his conduct towards them; but by establishing a system of espionage on all their movements, he surrounded them with snares, into which he was quite certain they would one day fall.

The Jesuits then, as now, were perfect masters of the secret system, but they could not have been more thoroughly adepts at all its internal machinery than was this Japanese Daimio; and very soon after his return to Yeddo, all the Spanish and Portuguese residents, their priests, and the native princes whom they had converted to their way of thinking, were surrounded by spies, who watched their goings out and comings in, crept into their most secret councils, and carried all the information so derived to Araki the Daimio of Hakoni. Did a wealthy native die, there were watchers beside his bed, with eyes and ears open to the counsels of his spiritual adviser, who seldom failed to persuade the dying man to hand over a considerable amount of his property to the keeping, and for the benefit of the Church; nor were spies wanting as well-concealed listeners when the Jesuit emissaries returned from some of their secret expeditions to the provinces—expeditions not wholly confined to religious matters, but having a very serious political tendency. Many of the great feudal princes of Japan were at that time discontented with the arbitrary rule of the upstart Taiko, who, by his extraordinary talent, had worked his way from a menial position into the place of his late master; and, not content with the portion of power that belonged to the Tycoon, he so completely absorbed that of the reigning Mikado,* that the latter was soon left with

* " The Mikado was, and is, the hereditary sovereign of the empire, descended from a long line of sovereigns of the same dynasty; a true sovereign in all the legal attributes of sovereignty, but having no power to act. Taiko Sama was a peasant's son, and favourite attendant of the actual generalissimo. He stripped the reigning Mikado

scarcely a nominal share in the government of the country over which he was the titular sovereign. The more despotic a monarch becomes, the more fearful is he of rivals near his throne; and inasmuch as the princes were discontented with the manner in which they were kept under by Taiko, so the latter became daily more uneasy at the wide extent of feudal power maintained by them.

The pomp and magnificence of the Romish clergy, and their influence over the aforementioned princes, alarmed his jealous nature; so, with all these suspicious fears rankling in his mind, he was only too ready to listen to the well-timed hints which Araki knew how to give: gradually, but surely, was the poison poured into his ear, turning the whole current of his feelings from amity to bitterness and wrath against the insidious foreigners. Nor was this all. His alarm was also awakened by the enormous amount of treasure in gold and silver which Araki reported as continually leaving his shores to enrich

of the last remnants of power. Since his time the Mikados are brought into the world, live, and die within the precincts of their court at Miaco, the boundaries of which they never pass during a whole lifetime. Their court is termed the Dairi."—See *Alcock's Capital of the Tycoon.*

the Europeans; and surely the quantity of foreign goods brought into the country seemed very small in proportion to the amount of precious metal given in exchange. Taiko was a far-sighted man, and, his eyes once opened by the revelations continually made to him, he became terrified at the probable consequences of allowing the foreigners to remain in his dominions. He had hitherto been led to understand that the desire of the Christian missionaries was to induce his people to worship the God and Creator whose dwelling was in the heavens; and, having himself studied the system of their religion, he did not disapprove of a creed that conveyed a sublime majesty of idea that coincided well with his own lofty mind. Like Agrippa, at one time he felt "almost persuaded" to be a Christian; but now things were set before him in a different light; and, having been favoured with a reading of certain epistles addressed by the Princes of Arima, Bungo, and Omara, to his Holiness the Pope of Rome, he from them learned that, if they did not *worship the Pope as God in heaven*, they were at least taught to *adore him as holding the place of God upon earth*, which was, in point of fact, making him and his subjects assume a position very closely resembling that of vassals to the proud Pontiff of Rome. Taiko Sama could not, and would not, draw a fine line of distinction between spiritual and temporal authority: in his eyes, one was synonymous with the other, and his proud heart rebelled against either—besides, as I said before, jealous as he was of his own nobility, he eagerly seized an opportunity that might lead to the humbling of their power also. We may imagine that any measures to ensure the latter effect would be far from meeting with support from the Daimio of Hakoni; indeed he began to fear that (to use a vulgar expression) he had considerably "overshot his mark:" *his* efforts were directed against the strangers who, like greedy parasites, were devouring all the wealth of the land, undermining old customs, and overturning the ancient religion of the country. To overthrow and exterminate *them* was the one great object for which he laboured; but even in the accomplishment of this, he was ever mindful to guard the interests of the mighty class to which he belonged. One rogue can easiest detect another, and such a deep schemer as Araki was not slow to read all the secret intentions of his chief, and to thwart those which did not suit his own views; and it is a certain fact, that Taiko Sama, with all his efforts, never succeeded in the chief desire of his heart,—to wit, the humbling of his own haughty nobles.

In the midst of his political intrigues, the Daimio of Hakoni, though continually diverted by more serious matters, never wholly forgot the disappointment which had so recently irritated his proud nature: indeed, Ama's rejection, instead of quenching his passion, only added fiercer fuel to the flame; and when, resting from court anxieties, and indulging in the solitary enjoyment of his favourite weed, his thoughts often wandered far away from Yeddo, to the beautiful vale of Abama, and there lingered over a well-remembered scene in the peaceful residence of Sako Miyako.

The Daimio's wives might now sigh in vain for a kindly smile from their lord, who entirely absented himself from their once-loved society, and lived wholly wrapt up in his own meditations. Among all the officers of the court, he mostly sought the companionship of Ama's brother; and using his own powerful interest in the young man's behalf, Tatish soon found himself advanced to a position of trust. But, alas! he little knew the grief which his new-found rank would cause him; for, bound by gratitude to his patron, he gradually became a mere tool in his hands. Regarding the Daimio with immense reverence himself, Tatish was amazed at his sister's folly in rejecting a man of his high rank and position; and he willingly undertook to exercise his influence, both with her and his father. But he was not prepared for all the difficulties he would have to encounter; for, continually occupied at court, he was as yet ignorant of the great changes that had taken place since he had last visited the home of his fathers. Judge then his surprise when, arriving with his attendants at the paternal mansion, he found neither Ama nor his parent in the house, it being the hour of evening prayer; and oh! what horror for the zealous young Pagan to discover that those he loved best were actually Christians, at that moment attending service in a Christian church endowed by themselves! This discovery placed the brother in a most painful position, for he foresaw all the danger it would bring upon those dearest to him; while to keep the matter secret would be utterly impossible; for well he knew that though he was trusted with a mission of confidence by the Daimio, some one of his attendants (hard to say which) was also employed to watch all his movements, and carefully report the same.

To Ama, her father, and the good Padre José Tatish was indeed the bearer of sad news; for he had to tell of the Siogun's sudden ill-feeling to the Christians, and the disastrous consequences likely to arise therefrom. He signified to his sister what unbounded influence Araki had with the Government, and how, if she would accept his offer, he would be certain to use that influence for the protection of her friends; in fact, he used every argument he could think of to induce her to yield, even hinting that his own life might be made a sacrifice to his master's rage, if again disappointed in the object on which he had so much set his heart. Ama's was indeed a pitiable position: hemmed in on all sides, not for a moment could she think of yielding to her brother's entreaties, yet heart-broken at the thought that her obduracy might probably bring destruction on him, her beloved father, and the good man who was to her as a second parent. From her own father she could receive no strengthening advice, for the old man seemed utterly bewildered, and incapable of thinking of what ought or ought not to be done; her brother had but one course of argument to offer, and could only see matters from one point of view; so Ama, in her despair, went to the good Padre, poured her sorrows into his sympathising ear, and asked his advice in this most distressing dilemma. His feelings coincided well with hers; and whatever might be the consequence, he would not counsel her to a step that would ensure her a life of misery, and draw upon her the fearful doom of an apostate from the Christian faith. On the contrary, he exhorted her to steadfastness, and led her to pray for guidance and faith to strengthen her in this time of need. And so the young girl, albeit with many tears, was again granted courage to give a final refusal to the suit of the proud Daimio of Hakoni.

It was with many a sad foreboding that the brave young officer of the Tycoon mounted his steed, to return again to the city; and heavy were the hearts, and tearful the eyes that watched him, as he rode away from the home into which he had brought so much sorrow, and which he was destined never to see again.

The court messengers had scarcely lost sight of
the vale of Abama before the gongs sounded through
the streets of its hamlets, and the Christian community established there assembled themselves in the
church, to hear the sad tidings lately brought
from the capital, and to discuss measures for their
future safety. Knowing how incapable they were of
self-defence, their weak hearts died within them as
they listened to the account of their dreaded Sovereign's wrath against the Christian religion; but
their good pastor, himself endowed with courage
from on high, earnestly exhorted them to banish
all fears, and trust in their heavenly Father, while,
on the other hand, if it were the Almighty will
that any of them should die for the Christian cause,
such martyrs would pass from this world to one of
greater beauty and happiness : and the good man's
countenance brightened with a holy radiance, as he
described the glories of the heavenly Paradise. So
the Christians of Abama, after holding sweet communion together, and strengthening each other to
steadfastness in the faith, returned to their peaceful
homes, to pursue the quiet routine of their daily
industry, uncertain each night as to what the dawn

might bring forth; and awaking each morning with anxieties for the day, that might have rendered them miserable but for their simple trust and steady reliance in the goodness of the All-powerful. With Ama, her father, and the good Padre José, it was a season of most anxious suspense, but one that drew them more closely to each other. Sako could not believe that his quondam friend would permit any measures likely to injure them; but the Padre knew the world better than he did. He had had much experience in the workings of the human passions; and knowing to what lengths even Christians may be led, if given over to their own corrupt natures, how much more dangerous an enemy must he prove who was under no restraint from fear of God, and whose high position gave him power to carry out any evil designs to which he might be prompted by a malicious and revengeful nature? In his heart the Padre José dreaded the worst, while Ama too trembled, as she remembered her own unaccountable sensation of fear, when under the influence of the dark Daimio's evil eye; that momentary terror had long ago passed away, but now, as it recurred to her mind, it assumed the form of a presentiment of evil,—an undefined shadow that, rising like a cloud, "no bigger than a man's hand," came as a dark spot on the hitherto bright horizon of her life, while it filled her with anxiety, the more intensely harrowing because of her inability to know whence, or in what form, the coming danger might appear. If she herself was the only person likely to be injured, her fears would have preyed less on her mind; but should the bolt fall on others,—on her father in his helpless old age, or her brave brother in the pride of his youth,—there was an agony in that thought that needed all Ama's Christian faith to sustain her in the thorny path on which she was about to enter.

CHAPTER VII.

―――

NOTHING could exceed Araki's rage and disappointment, when he received Ama's decided and final answer; yet, to judge from his countenance, no one could have suspected that a tumult of angry passions disturbed his inmost soul:—only by the quivering lip, the deadly paleness, and, above all, the malign expression of his eye, could a bystander perceive how much and how variously he was moved. Even these emotions were but transient; for he did not choose

to let Tatish know how angry he felt at his sister's
conduct, lest the young man, guided by instincts of
affection for his relatives, might set himself to coun-
teract certain designs which he had hastily formed
against them. I say "hastily," for but a dim outline
of their nature darted through his mind; it would take
much anxious thought and calm deliberation to carry
them into full effect. With Tatish continually about
the court, it would be impossible to accomplish any of
his purposes, while the young man's open destruction
would not be a likely means of winning his sister's
regard: better far to do him an apparent service, by
getting him appointed to some high office that would
take him far away from Yeddo, and still farther from
his home.

It is said that Fortune favours the brave, but too
often she is equally kind to the bad; for she soon fell
in with, and opened a way for the execution of Araki's
sinister designs.

Taiko Sama, being at this time horrified at the
number of Christians to be found in the muster-roll
of his immense army, determined to give them something else to do besides hearing masses, and swelling
the pomp of religious processions. With this intent,

he hastily summoned them from all parts of the
empire, with orders to prepare for immediate and
active service, hoping that the dangers of the battle-
field and the hardships of the camp might rid him
of a few of his Christian soldiers. According to
the learned Titsingh, the Japanese of those mediæval
times were a military people, by no means unskilled
in military arts and tactics, while in personal bravery
they were unsurpassed by the most warlike nations
of India. From their infancy they were instructed
from books recording the heroic deeds of their ancestors, and so filled with a national importance and
love of glory that led them to make the art of war
a favourite study; and, Christians though many of
them were, their Emperor had reason to be proud of
the noble army that left his shores,—one part bound
for China, and the other for the Korean peninsula.
Innumerable were the hardships to be encountered
by those brave soldiers, during their wearisome march
by land, and perilous voyage over the treacherous
waters that bound the Japanese islands; and though
their arms were finally victorious over the enemy,
few of them ever saw their native shores again. It
being Araki's object to get Tatish out of the way,

F

he mentioned his name to the Emperor, as most fitted (from his well-known talent and personal valour) to be entrusted with the command of a regiment bound for the war. It was an honourable post for so young a man; and Tatish, burning with military zeal, and longing to rival the great exploits of his forefathers, was delighted at the career so unexpectedly opened to him, while he was overwhelmed with gratitude at what he deemed unexampled kindness on the part of his patron. True, he longed to be allowed to visit his home before setting out on his march; but, either designedly or otherwise, he was kept so closely to his military preparations that not a day's absence could be granted either to him or his brother officers, whose brave hearts were saddened at being obliged to leave their native country without one word of farewell to those they loved. The native Christians in the army being thus disposed of, the enemies of the Cross did not long allow those left behind to remain in peace: daily, hourly was the Emperor's wrath stirred up against them and the European settlers, whose grasping, over-reaching conduct in mercantile matters was but too faithfully reported at court, while their very sayings were carried to the Tycoon, and very often misinterpreted for their destruction, until at last his hatred of the foreigners reached a culminating point that placed it beyond control ; and regarding them, and their priests, as traitors, seeking to undermine his government by stealing away the hearts of his people, he determined to drive them out of his dominions. Soon Christian Japan was electrified by the issue of a royal decree, ordering the immediate banishment of the European traders, their priests, and all connected with them ; while the natives were forbidden, under the severest pains and penalties, to continue the observances of the Christian religion. This first blow was the signal for every other outrage. With fanatic fury the Pagan Japanese rushed into the churches ; tore down and trampled upon the crosses ; razed the sacred edifices to the ground ; demolished the dwellings, schools, hospitals, and every other building connected with the foreigners ; and even further wreaking their vengeance by violating the Christians' graves.

Of course, this revolution was first felt at the capital, but from thence it rapidly spread itself into the provinces, causing a universal panic all over the land ; and soon Sako Yoriama, the Japanese merchant at Simoda, found himself deserted by his Portuguese friends, who, in terror for their lives and property, at the very first alarm collected their wealth together and sailed for Firando, where they hoped to be allowed to remain until the Tycoon's rage against them was in some measure abated. The wealthy churchmen followed the example of their flock, and all tried to persuade Yoriama to accompany them in their flight; but the young merchant was slow to exile himself from his native country while those nearest and dearest to him were in such imminent danger; yet he, too, gathered his capital together in readiness for the worst, and, well knowing what that might be, he invested a portion of his wealth in the purchase of a ship, which he ordered to be ready for sailing by the time of his return from a visit to his father's home. At that period the Japanese ships, though built on the plan of the Chinese junks, were not such as they are now; but being large, stoutly built craft, manned by bold experienced sailors, they were quite equal to weathering the fury of oceanic tempests. That they made very slow progress, we may imagine from the fact, that the Japanese ambassadors to the Pope of Rome, who left their country when all were peacefully inclined to the Christian religion, passed *eight years* in going and coming back; so that when they again returned home, accompanied by the Jesuit superior, Père Valignani, the edicts of banishment had been issued, Christianity wrecked, and the face of things altogether changed.

We may imagine what a sad, as well as unexpected, blow this was to the Christian missionary, and the native Christian princes whose sojourn in Europe had been one long ovation ; for, not only were they sumptuously entertained at the court of the Romish Pontiff, but also at those European courts whose sovereigns owed allegiance to the spiritual sway of Rome. The princes of Arima, Bungo, and Omara stood in high favour with the late Diogoun, " Nobunnanga," and it was with his best wishes, and under his happiest auspices, that they had sailed for the (to them unknown) regions of the West; now returning to their native land they expected a glad welcome from their new sovereign (who had begun his reign by favouring the Christians), instead of which, they found themselves, not only proscribed on account of their religious faith, but even suspected of being leagued with foreigners in a political enterprise dangerous to the temporal power of Japan.

Alas! for the stability of human expectations. Those Japanese princes, in all the weary months during which they had braved the perils of the deep, suffering untold miseries while tossed on oceanic waves in their heavy lumbering junks, must have found some comfort in the anticipation of enlightening their fellow-countrymen, and introducing to them the many new customs, arts, and improvements which had caught their fancy during their visit to civilized Europe; but no sooner had the travellers reached their still beloved "Land of the Rising Sun," than all their cherished aërial castles crumbled before their eyes, for not only was the religion imported from Europe fallen into disrepute, but Europeans, and everything European, or otherwise foreign, was tabooed by a watchful and jealously awakened government.

CHAPTER VIII.

———

" 'Tis hard ; but when we needs must bear,
  Enduring patience makes the burden light."
CREECH.

WHEN the merchant of Simoda reached his father's
home, he found the vale of Abama as yet undisturbed by the devastating hand of the Pagan fanatics.
True, rumours like the rumbling of distant thunder
had often caused the Christian community to tremble
for the safety of their beloved church, and still more
beloved pastor, who daily went from house to house
comforting the faint-hearted, and encouraging the

weak ones of his charge; he had turned a deaf ear to the warning entreaties of his brother priests, who, like hireling shepherds as they were, when they saw the wolf coming (or rather when they heard his angry howl in the distance), not caring for the sheep, but caring only for themselves, fled, and left their flocks to be scattered abroad.

It was a plain fact that many of the Romish churchmen had undertaken the proselyting mission to Japan more with a view to enrich themselves than to turn a heathen people from darkness to light, and we find that those who were actuated by such mundane motives were proud and arrogant in the days of prosperity, and proved themselves cowards in the hour of danger; for, wholly loving the world and greedy of worldly gain, though they deceived others by their fair show of religious fervour, they had not succeeded in so fully deceiving themselves as to conceive that the God whose holy service they had so profaned would be to them a sheltering Father in the hour of trial: so having none to trust to on earth, and not daring to rely on heavenly protection, they took themselves off with those who had aided and abetted them in their evil courses. Yet all did not

fly, for history records the fact that twenty-six priests
yielded their lives as martyrs to the cause of Christianity. Sako Yoriama had been the bearer of mes-
sages to the Padre José, from his brethren at Simoda.
To these the good man paid very little attention; but,
though fearless for himself, he was keenly anxious for
the safety of his patron and that patron's beautiful
daughter, and he shuddered to think of what might
be her fate if left to the mercies of the officers of
the Tycoon, who, though sent nominally for the purpose of uprooting and eradicating the Christian religion,
would probably be entrusted with other orders by the
proud Daimio whose advances Ama had so decidedly
rejected.

It was very difficult to persuade old Sako to leave
the beautiful home where he had passed a long and
peaceful life : his mind, blunted by the infirmities of
age, could scarcely comprehend a necessity for his
doing so, for he still maintained his faith in Araki's
friendship, believing that in him he would find a
protector instead of an enemy. With Ama the case
was different : she saw too well that danger threatened
them, and, grieved though she was to leave her beloved valley, still to her anything was better than

falling into the hands of the dark Daimio of Hakoni. But the Padre, would not he go too? They had plenty for all; for, besides Yoriama's own property, his father's yearly income of 50,000 kokous of rice, when transferred into hard cash, would produce by no means a despicable sum: and who so welcome to share in their good things of this world as he who had taught them the road to eternal happiness in the next? But the Padre was not to be tempted, and with much grief his friends found him steadfast in his determination to remain at Abama; for, in assuring them that it was their duty to fly and save their lives, he as strongly insisted that his own duty was to remain at his post and comfort those poor members of his flock who, unable to leave their humble homes, would naturally look to him for support in the hour of trial. In leaving Abama, it was necessary for Miyako and his daughter to act with the utmost secrecy and caution, only confiding their intentions to those of their attendants on whose fidelity they could rely, being like themselves converts to the faith. These were well provided with arms for the protection of the party, and they each took a solemn vow to sacrifice their very lives in the defence of their master and his daughter, for, the better to avoid any encounter with the emissaries of the Tycoon, it would be necessary to travel on the most unfrequented roads, over rocky hills, and through pathless forests, fraught with dangers of their own, being constantly infested by wild animals and hordes of lawless Lonins. Fortunately their journey would not be as long as it was perilous, for the blue waters of the ocean were visible from all the higher ground about Abama; and by that sea-coast, near a little quiet fishing village, Yoriama's ship would await their coming, it being deemed more prudent to embark from that obscure place than to venture on a longer though easier journey to the more public port of Simoda. Two of Ama's handmaids were desirous of accompanying their mistress; but the third,—would they had never confided their intentions to the faithless Orra, who, beguiling them with many protestations of affectionate fidelity, was really a spy on their movements, paid by and devotedly attached to the interests of the Daimio of Hakoni. Slily did this deceitful girl wander about the house, playing the eavesdropper on every possible occasion; and though she had not been entrusted with the exact plan of their intended journey, she acquired a great deal of information on the subject, and finally, before their preparations were completed, she secretly left the place, and with an accomplice in the village, whom she paid to act as her attendant and carry her musical instrument, in the disguise of a public singer she set out for Yeddo; and there we leave her to complete her evil devices, while we remain at Abama, following the Christians in their rapidly changing fortunes.

CHAPTER IX.

———

"Lo! where the crucified Christ, from His cross is gazing upon you!
  See! in those sorrowful eyes, what meekness, and holy compassion!
  Hark! how those lips still repeat the prayer, 'O Father, forgive them!'
  Let us repeat that prayer, in the hour when the wicked assail us;
  Let us repeat it now, and say, 'O Father, forgive them!'"

LONGFELLOW.

A LITTLE more than a year has passed by since we first introduced our readers to "The Land of the Rising Sun." Since that time weeks and months have rolled away, each successive period opening on events of the highest importance to the great Island Empire of the East; I say of the *highest* importance, for not only have they wrought great *political* changes in the country, but they have still further involved the everlasting welfare of millions of human souls.

It is summer; a glorious season everywhere, but more than ever lovely in that rich and pleasant land, where the queen of night, smiling softly on the landscape, shows us a scene of Arcadian beauty, not unlike that so exquisitely described by a Transatlantic bard in his rich word-painting of "Evangeline." " Peace seems to reign upon earth," and peculiarly peaceful is the vale of Abama, sleeping in its calm retirement of rural grandeur. A few hours ago "the great Sun looked with the eye of love" on a busy picture of agricultural life, bespeaking the prosperous industry of a simple happy people, among whom none are rich, and none have ever felt the bitter pangs of want. *Then* a noisy hum denoted the presence of busy men, and a still greater proportion of busy women and children, who at this season are always actively engaged in rural labours; but now all is silence. Every peasant has retired to his home, to enjoy his frugal supper of rice or fish, accompanied by their favourite beverages of tea or saki; all is still in the hamlet below: even the barber's whistle* is no longer heard, for the old blind man

---

* In all the Japanese towns and villages there are regular professors of the shampooing art; and sometimes these are barbers. The

has gone his rounds; and even those who could not
afford the benefit of an artistic shampooing at his
hands, have long since enjoyed a hot bath* to refresh
them after the labours of the day. Yes, all is quiet:
the calm stillness is only occasionally broken by the
wild birds' cry as they fly in flocks over the valley,
disturbing the composure of the solemn stork, who
rises with a discontented scream from the neighbourhood of some pond, or rippling mountain torrent,
where he has been indulging in a little moonlight
fishing for eels and dissipated frogs. Yes, all is
silent now: no human voices are heard, but the canine
race still keep up their perpetual bark, varied occasionally by a prolonged howl, as some dismal individual feels inspired with melancholy, induced by his
solitary contemplation of the moon's pale face. But,
hark! another sound is heard, another voice is borne

blind, too (of whom there are many in Japan), often· adopt it as
a means of livelihood, and go about the streets in the evening,
whistling to attract the attention of their customers.

* The Japanese are a very cleanly people; the poorest labourer
has his hot bath every night before retiring to rest. May we not
recommend this feature of their character to the attention of some of
the Celtic denizens of our own British isles? but, alas! we fear that
our friends in the sister isle, to say nothing of those among the
Cambrian hills, and Caledonian wilds, would refuse to listen to the
voice of the barber, were he to whistle never so wisely.

softly on the still night air,—a sweet-toned voice, that speaks to the hearts of the simple villagers, who one by one, and in groups of two and three, leave their homes, and wend their way up the valley and along the lane that leads to the Christian church. Silently and sadly, anxiously they go, for they have heard rumours of threatening dangers, and they have now been summoned to join the household of Sako Miyako at the midnight mass, when prayers are to be offered for their especial benefit in the little church that has been endowed by them. All the neighbouring peasantry hold their land under Sako: he has ever been just and generous to his people, and now that he and his daughter are going from them they know not what may be their future fate. True, he has left his property in the hands of one who will be bound to give an account of the same; but will he, the steward, be careful of their interest, or may he not rather be tempted to advance his own at their expense?

Soon the sacred edifice is well-nigh full; and as we glance among the motley groups we see many a fair face, and some that would have been passing fair, had not their ideas of conjugal duty obliged

them to blacken their teeth, varnish their lips, and
pick out the last hairs of their eyebrows, thereby
(with the best intentions) marring the beauty of nature's handiwork.* These black-mouthed females are
all matrons, and not a few of them are encumbered by
little nude brown babies, whose sharp eyes peep know-
ingly from the sack, or pocket in which they are
slung on their mother's backs. Here and there a stal-
wart father is sole guardian of a little one, and said
father, albeit he is now a Christian, shows tokens on
his scantily draped figure of recent acquaintance with
Paganism, for every visible morsel of skin is decorated with flying dragons, animals, and other strange
devices, tattooed with bright blue paint, in a very
artistic, but not less singular manner. Many of
these poor creatures are still intensely ignorant, but
while we smile at their grotesque appearance, we
cannot but admire their earnest countenances, the pious
devotion of their behaviour, and the expression of

---

* The Japanese matrons deem it right to sacrifice all their beauty
on the altar of conjugal fidelity; they blacken their teeth and pluck
out the last hairs of their eyebrows, on purpose to disfigure their
faces and prove that they have no desire to captivate other admirers.
This is no doubt a very laudable motive on their part, but we
would scarcely recommend its practice to our English friends.

G

love that beams in every eye that is directed to their good pastor. It was his especial desire thus to gather his little congregation round him, ere they should be divided, never more to meet together for worship under one roof. Yes, never more in this world, for the time of trial was already come, and soon the fairest of his flock would be driven away by the threats of the angry wolf; and as the good Padre, glancing round the assembled congregation, found his eye dwelling for a moment on the beautiful Ama, kneeling beside her grey-haired sire, one short spasm of agony passed through his heart, as he remembered that it was probably the last time that he should ever see her there. Intensely acute were the feelings that almost convulsed his frame while he wrestled in silent prayer ere the commencement of the service; but when he arose from his knees the anguished lines had left his face, a calm expression of holy resignation illumined every feature, and not until the close of his pulpit exhortation did his faltering voice again prove that, though the spirit was willing, the flesh was weak. Pure and unadulterated were the Christian doctrines which that good priest impressed upon his flock; true, he belonged to the vitiated Church

of Rome; when in Europe he had scrupulously obeyed
her dictates, bowed to her authority, and acknowledged the infallible supremacy of her Pontiff; but
now, in this far off land, cut off from his more bigoted,
but less earnest brethren, left free to think for himself, and to enjoy silent communion with nature, and
nature's God, his religious views underwent a puri-
fying process, and though he still nominally adhered
to the Church in which he had been educated, his
was the pure faith of the Apostles, and he preached
the pure Gospel to his people, teaching them to
adore the one true God, and to trust for eternal
salvation solely to the merits of His Son, who was
crucified as an atoning sacrifice for the sins of the
whole world. Often had he impressed these saving
truths upon them, but never more earnestly than now,
when some of them being about to leave him, his
heart told him he then addressed them for the last
time.

The last time! How like a tolling bell is the
sound of those few words!—A bell that stirs up
painful recollections in almost every heart; for who is
the favoured mortal, who cannot recall some agoniz-
ing memory of—a last time? Be it the mourner whose

heart has wept over a bereavement that has left him desolate; his sorrow may have long since passed away, time may have healed his wounds, still, do they not sometimes bleed afresh when accident, or circumstance, recalls the memory of that silent hour when he gazed for the *last time* on the beloved features, " so fair, so calm, so softly sealed" in death? Yet death is not the only source of sorrow, his is not the only hand that turns our hour-glass for the *last time*. Nay, some have met, and have parted, in full hopes of another, and perhaps a happier meeting, and so they closed that last interview, and being ignorant of the future they were thus spared the indescribable heart-ache; but has it not since been felt with tenfold bitterness? for now when all is past, words and looks, circumstances, of little import in themselves, become replete with harrowing interest, when associated with the memory of *that last time*. The Padre José had passed a checkered life, — checkered by sin and sorrow; he had gazed for the *last ttme* on the fair lineaments of one whom his guilt had brought to an early grave. He could recall the *last time* that an aged mother, had with dying lips besought him to repent and turn from his evil ways; he could re-

member when from the deck of the outward-bound
ship he looked for the *last time*, as the shores of his
native land receded from his yearning gaze; he could
remember all these bygone sorrows, yet never had his ,
heart ached with anguish more intense than when, in
that one brief glance at the beautiful Ama, the
thought flashed across his mind, that now, for the
last time, he and she were about to worship together,
and that ere the morning dawned he would lay
his hand in parting benediction on that fair young
head. Was his, then, only a fatherly affection
for the gentle girl, who with childlike innocence
had confided to him all her joys and sorrows, all her
spiritual fears and doubts? He was her first teacher,
he had found her in ignorance, her mind darkened
by Pagan superstition, her very reasoning faculties
benumbed for want of exercise. Like a fair piece
of sculpture, her face and form were faultless, but
there was a something wanting, a something without
which the most perfect beauty is but as cold dead
marble; to the Padre's lot it fell to supply that
something, for he it was that first awakened all the
powers of her inquiring mind, and turned her
thoughts from "ignoble things" to the highest aim

of human existence. Not immediately had this change
been wrought, the light of knowledge had gradually
illumined her dark understanding, while her teacher
watched the dawning of awakened intellect with the
same anxious pleasure as that shown by a careful
gardener when he sees fresh beauties unfold from
the opening bud of some new, and precious rose.
Alone in the world, and of a naturally affectionate
disposition, his love for Ama had become a part of
his being, and if uninterrupted it might thus have
gone on for ever, he calmly content to live and die
near her, and to have had her to close his eyes in
the last trying hour; but now he was rudely awakened
from his happy trance, and suddenly made aware
of the full extent of his feelings, while combined
with his great heart-sorrow, was the humiliating grief
that even in thought, he had been unfaithful to his
priestly vows. His was now a tender conscience,
tender towards God and man, and he trembled at the
least dereliction from the rugged path he had chosen
for himself, when in much penitence and sorrow he
had taken up his cross, and torn himself away from
the land of his fathers, snapping every home affection,
and breaking every last remaining link that bound

him to earthly ties; resigning the inheritance that
had descended to him from a long line of ancestors,
giving up his wealth, as some restitution to those
whom he had wronged by youthful errors, and poor
as the poorest of his brethren,—poor even as those
humble peasants who were the first chosen apostolic
missionaries,—the once rich and gay "Don José de
Sebina" laid aside his worldly rank, and gave up all
worldly considerations for the sake of that soul whose
eternal safety he had perilled by a reckless life of
folly and of sin. As the Padre José he embraced
the cause of Christ; and, animated by an earnest
desire to devote himself, body and soul, to His service, he determined to spend the remainder of his
days in propagating the Gospel among the Pagan
natives of the newly opened island empire of the
East. While following the course he had marked
out for himself, he fully believed that philanthropic
affection for the whole human race was the only love
that could now find admission to his heart. Yet so
deceptive is the human heart, that even he who watches
himself most closely, and submits to the most scru-
tinising self-examination, is sometimes doomed to find
that by himself he has been most cruelly deceived.

Who can tell how deeply the sudden discovery of his weakness affected the Padre, or how much it increased the sorrow of his soul, when, torn by contending feelings, the flesh, wrestling with the spirit, uttered "the vain and selfish sigh" that testified a longing for the joys of an earthly home, where one fair being would be his alone, and one fond heart would love him best? But soon the sigh is stifled, the heart agony has passed away, and the spirit, strengthened by prayer, clings with loving helplessness to the Cross; and so, the hour of temptation over, the Christian soldier resolves to abide by his banner, and (if necessary) to lay down his life in its defence.

That night he accompanied Sako Miyako and his family a little way on their journey, and, bidding them "God speed," he returned to Abama, a sorrow-stricken lonely man—lonely, yet not alone; for in the solitude of his heart he turned still more eagerly to "Him who dwells on high," who "*knows all, yet loves us better than He knows.*"

CHAPTER X.

———

LET us away to Yeddo, and see how events are
there developing, from the intricate meshes of one
evil mind. In a private room of his great mansion,
we behold Araki the Daimio busily engaged in the
mysteries of the toilet—not that he is giving himself
any trouble about it; he is merely submitting, while
his attendants attire him in the complicated folds of
his court dress. The Daimio seems in good temper

this morning; his countenance wears an expression almost benign, for has he not just had the parting adieus of the brave Tatish, and seen him (with the noble body of troops under his command) pass through the city, the sunshine glistening on the gilded helmets and silver scaled vests of the officers, as, in all the pomp of martial array, they started on their march for the Korea? It was a goodly sight for any one to behold; but especially pleasant to the Daimio, who, now that Tatish was out of the way, is left free to carry out his designs on the family at Abama. His mind is full of these thoughts, as he prepares to attend the court; but can it indeed be Araki who is now leaving the room, trying to walk with his usual pomposity; but the dignity of his movements, considerably impeded by the grotesquely awkward costume in which he is arrayed, not by his own choice, but by the conventional rules of court etiquette, which, in the "Land of the Rising Sun," are even as pitiless as in this more favoured land of ours? We have described the Daimio before; but it seems almost impossible to convey an idea of his appearance, when in his full court dress. Let us, however, imagine (if we can) a figure not unlike a mammoth insect, for the shoulders of the kami-shimo (or upper vest) are extended so as to give the appearance of huge expanded wings, while the silk trousers (being lengthened beyond all needful proportion, and allowed to trail on the ground for a yard or so behind the wearer), bear a very close resemblance to a tail. Feet, the creature has apparently none; yet he walks, or rather shuffles along, but that he does not come to grief by falling on his face, is a matter of much wonder to us, the un-initiated. But practice (even as it enables our courtly dames to back out of the presence of royalty without becoming entangled in their trains) enables the Japanese Daimio to walk about with his feet in what appear to be the knees of his nether garments, and we may be quite certain that he will reach the royal presence without making even one faux-pas. His mysterious toilet completed, he is leaving the room; but just as he reaches the door, a shadow crosses the sunbeam that streams in at the open window, while a female voice is heard singing in a rather monotonous, but softly sweet tone. The voice, more than the song, arrests the Daimio's steps; but, as he listens to the words, they too seem to have an unusual and startling effect; for, hastily dismissing his attendants, he advances to the window. There, half concealed by the branches of a beautiful cryptomeria, stands a tall, showy-looking girl, who returns (with interest) the Daimio's bold glance of admiration; she does not appear to be a stranger to him; on the contrary, he meets her in the familiar manner of an old acquaintance, and, after the first interchange of salutations, they retire together to a solitary grotto that ornaments a shady corner of the garden. What passed in that interview, we cannot tell, for neither human eye nor human ear were present to assist us in recording the words spoken; we can only say, that though the time was short, high words must have closed the "tête-à-tête," for, as the Daimio left the singing girl, his countenance wore an angry, troubled expression, while she, throwing after him a handful of golden coins, with a gesture of indignant rage, rushed from the garden, with angry words on her lips, and her bold black eyes flashing with a fury that seemed to tell of mortified passion and malignant hate. Aye, in her the Daimio had chosen a weapon to his own destruction; for while, for his own purposes, desirous of flattering

her vanity, he had awakened in her passionate nature
a wild affection for himself, by which alone she had
been prompted to undertake a long and perilous
journey, that she might bring him the promised information as to the proceedings of the household of
Sako Miyako. But, either wilfully or otherwise, she had
delayed too long; and, as Araki calculated the time
spent on the road, he trembled with rage to think
that his prey must have already escaped, and that
she for whom he had so long plotted and schemed
was probably, even now, far beyond his reach. Better
had Orra never come, than come too late; besides
she could not, or would not, tell with certainty what
road the fugitives were to take, for it was not her
desire to send the Daimio hurrying after them; on
the contrary, she had hoped that, when he found
Ama totally out of his power, he would give up all
thought of her, and (in pity, if nothing else) bestow
upon Orra the affection she so ardently coveted, and
for which she had perilled so much. But she reckoned
without her host; Araki was not a wavering youth,
but a determined, middle-aged man; he loved Ama
with all the strength of his nature, and the more
difficulties he found in his way, the more determined

was he to surmount them all; and, cost him what it might, he would never rest until he had won the daughter of Sako Miyako to be his willing, or unwilling bride. With the discovery of Orra's passion for himself, came doubts as to whether she had acted with integrity in the matter; so the misguided girl, instead of receiving the reward she desired, was only loaded with reproaches and stinging sarcasms, and when she tearfully alluded to all the perils and expenses she had endured in his behalf, she was offered a handful of gold, when a kind word would have been ten times more precious. The sweetest sweets make the strongest acids; so, in a passionate, ill-governed nature, love repulsed begets the deadliest hate, and from the moment that they parted from their conference in that cool, well-shaded grotto, Araki the Daimio had no more bitter foe than Orra, the homeless minstrel, who, after frequenting and becoming the chief ornament of all the tea-houses at Yeddo, contrived to entangle the affections of a powerful prince, possessing, as it happened, a large territory contiguous to Hakoni, while with him and his brother Daimio (as formerly with our northern Gaelic chiefs), being near neighbours did not make

them close friends; on the contrary, they were continually quarrelling when at their country houses, and
were bitter rivals when at court.

The position of a Court favourite is always one of
peculiar peril; for even the most just and honest are
sure to possess many enemies, who, envying the talent
or good fortune which has raised them to their high
pinnacle of trust, are ever on the watch for some
unguarded action, some faux pas, that may haply tend
to their downfall. Now Araki, though talented, was
neither so just nor so honest (especially in his present
line of conduct) as to live *sans peur et sans reproche;*
arbitrary too, and tyrannical to those below him, he
was very far from being a popular man, even with
his political clique; while the marked favour with
which he was treated by the Tycoon only served to
create a jealous hatred among the rest of his com-
peers. Altogether, while of enemies he had many,
friends he had none : his was not the nature to seek
for, or to inspire friendship, for those who were his
inferiors feared him; his equals hated him; and even
his Sovereign, who prized the diplomatic abilities of
his minister, and believed in the attachment he had
always shown to himself and his government, was of

too suspicious a disposition to place full confidence in him, or any one of those proud hereditary princes over whose heads he had risen to the supreme power. Yet he treated the Daimio of Hakoni more as a friend than as a subject; for in *his* high aspiring mind he often found a kindred spirit—a spirit that, under other circumstances and under different influences, might have made its possessor a blessing, instead of a curse to his fellow-men. As it was, the usually wily, cautious noble was so madly led away by the one all-absorbing motive, that he had not even sense to perceive that contriving his own absence from the court, was, at that season especially, about the most impolitic step that he could take; but so eager, so hurried was he to prosecute the object which he had in view, that he forgot all other considerations, even turning his back on Yeddo; while Orra, in her disappointed love and longing for vengeance, was allowed to wander at will in the haunts of his greatest foes, to tell them the secrets of his heart, and give them the key to that suddenly active zeal which had created surprise in every one about the court of the Tycoon.

CHAPTER XI.

ARAKI having sought and obtained a private audience with the Emperor, laid before him the startling intelligence that the rich territory of Abama was not only a hot-bed of Christianity, but also that its inhabitants were disaffected towards his sacred person, and ready at any moment to join with other seditious provinces in an endeavour to subvert the government of the country. Taiko's mind being at the time in a continual state of fermentation against the Christians, this news caused his wrath to explode

H

with all the energy of a powder magazine that has been suddenly ignited by a fiery spark; yet in all his anger he issued no death-warrants against his own people; for though Araki was given full authority to proceed at once to Abama, accompanied by a chosen body of soldiers, and Yakonins, it was rather to terrify the natives into submission, and compel them to renounce the dangerous creed they had embraced, than to destroy their lives or injure their property. With any foreigners, priests or laymen, the case would be widely different; for they had been given six months to take themselves out of the country; that time had now elapsed, and any found within the Japanese monarch's dominions would assuredly forfeit their lives.

We may imagine with what alacrity Araki undertook his commission to Abama; indeed, as we see him leaving Yeddo, at the head of a body of troops and fierce Samourai,* we can hardly believe that he is the same man who a few hours ago left his mansion on a visit of ceremony to the palace of the Tycoon. Then, even eyes the most impartial could detect little manly beauty in the grotesque figure

---

* Samourai, or Yakonins,—Japanese police.

which, (like the clown in the pantomime,) looked all the queerer for the excessively grave, and solemn dignity, with which its owner took his place on the top of his high horse; a silken bridle grasped in each hand, while an armed attendant walked at either side of the saddle, (from which he seemed every moment about to fly), two more in advance, carefully, and cautiously, leading on the steed. *Then* he looked like an equestrian actor in a masquerade, receiving the first lesson in his part; *now,* attired in a more befitting costume, his countenance all alive with excitement, and the outlines of his fine figure set off by a dress that at least has nothing ridiculous in its arrangement, he does not require to be almost held on his saddle by the attendant grooms; indeed he seems to be perfect master of the vicious, fiery brute on which he is mounted, whose abnormal tendencies of rearing and biting being checked by a superior force, he is fain to content himself by occasionally lashing out with his hind legs, in a manner not at all conducive to the comfort, or safety, of those who are following. Fierce, villanous looking individuals, those followers are, and consequently the better suited to the pur-

pose for which Araki has selected them from the
government troops at Yeddo. It is not the first
time that they have been called out against the
Christians; the ruins of many a church and monastery give evidence to the energy of their destructive
hate, while like wild ware-wolves, having once
steeped their hands in Christian blood, they are
only too eager to enjoy the same exciting game
again. Yet of all this Taiko knows nothing; he
believes that his government, even his life is in
danger, through the machinations of the Christians;
he also believes implicitly in the good faith of
Araki, the Daimio of Hakoni; for he knows not
that other motives besides steadfast loyalty have
combined to increase his hatred to Christianity, and
his active zeal in its extermination. Taiko Sama was
a clever man, skilled in the exercise of worldly
wisdom; yet even his discerning eyes could not read
the thoughts of the human heart: for only to One,
the Being whose very existence was denied by that
proud Pagan Tycoon, are "all hearts open, and all
desires known."

CHAPTER XII.

———

".   .   .   .   .   Have a care
Of whom you talk, to whom, and what, and where."
POOLEY.

THAT was a bright summer day on which Araki, with his band of destructive Samourai, dashed through the streets of Yeddo, startling the peacefully disposed inhabitants, and causing them no small amount of consternation; for only very urgent duty indeed could warrant their riding at such a pace through the city. A few years ago such a sight as an armed body of troops galloping furiously through the capital would have given rise to no small amount of anxious surmise; but now strange things were happening every day, and though (like the constantly recurring earthquakes) the frequency of the shocks deprived them of much of their novelty, it did not render them one whit less terrific. When the foreigners first appeared in Japan the people watched their movements with a good deal of jealous anxiety, but that feeling passed away when they found that, instead of being aggressive foes, they only preserved the harmless demeanour of quiet merchants; their religion, too, was of a peaceful nature; and, as yet, the lower orders could not understand why the strangers had been so suddenly driven from the country; and while many of them still sympathised with the Christians, they trembled lest the destination of this armed force might have something to do with them. Not loudly did they express their fears, for the system of espionage employed by the Japanese government renders every man cautious as to what he says, and to who he confides his opinion: one family in every four being appointed secretly to watch over their neighbours, and report to others who are watching over them, and so on in every gradation of the

social scale, until you reach the palace itself. Even
there it does not end, for one official watches over
another; and the Emperor himself can scarcely be
said to be a free agent. But Taiko-Sama, however
he shackled the words and actions of others, took care
to preserve his own freedom intact; and even if he
suffered himself to be biassed by the opinions of some
of his nobles, he took every measure to make those
feudal chiefs keenly sensible of his despotic authority.
As I said before, he placed the most implicit faith in
Araki, and yet instinct taught him to fear a nature so
similar to his own; and while he trusted the Daimio
of Hakoni more than any of his nobles, he was always
on his guard against anything like encroachment on
his part; so that even on this mission to Abama
(when the Daimio, having selected his men from the
government troops and his own most tried retainers,
might have fancied himself perfectly safe) he was
watched by one in his train, who would be careful
to note all his movements, and repeat them at the
palace. But, interested as we are in his proceedings, we must e'en follow him on his road. Never
has the city of the Tycoons appeared to greater
advantage than on this summer afternoon; even the

gloomy moated houses of the official quarters look
bright and cheery, as the sun shines on the armorial
bearings that decorate their high-peaked roofs; everywhere the city is alive, gay, and stirring; the bazaars
thronged with groups of merry folk, all actively intent
on buying and selling; and though a fire has the
night before laid the whole side of a street in ashes,
the destructive casualty seems to produce little effect
on the passers-by, as they hurry to enjoy their usual
gossip in the public baths; where men and women
meet daily, to perform their ablutions, and discuss
all private and political affairs of the nation. As
the horsemen clatter down the street the gossips for
a moment desert their various employments, and
return again to hazard many a vague conjecture, and
speculate on the state of things in general.

Utterly regardless of every one, with hearts un-
cheered by the lively scenes through which they pass,
and eyes closed to the natural beauties of the great
city, the horsemen ride on through leagues of streets,
causing confusion to the children, and dogs, who tumble
over one another, as in terror they clear out of the way
of that grim dark troop. On, on, they go; caring
nothing for the beautiful scenery around them; never

seeing the sunbeams as they dance on the blue waters
of the bay, nor the temple-crowned hills, whose well-
wooded slopes are fringed with every variety of
evergreen, and flowery shrub.

As soon as Yeddo has faded in the distance Araki
draws up his men, and gives them their marching
orders. They are to make no delays on the road;
only halting for refreshment, when compelled by
actual necessity, on reaching Abama they are not
to cause any stir in the village, but proceed as quietly
as possible to the home of Sako Miyako (who he
represents as a Christian, leagued with the foreigners
for the destruction of the national government and
religion of Japan), to surround it, and take him and
his family prisoners; but not one hair of their heads
is to be injured, or the slightest disrespect shown to
any of them, on pain of instant death. These orders,
given in a voice that awes even those fierce men, the
Daimio, as he rides on, again relapses into his usual
dignified silence. It was a long and rough journey
to Abama; but only once were the party allowed to
sleep on the road, and that was on the last night of
their march; then with the earliest dawn, before the
sun's first mild glow had faded from the landscape,

they again pursued their way, startling many a peasant who, proceeding peaceably to his morning work, was fain to lie down and hide himself in the nearest thicket, rather than encounter the fierce Samourai. Terror and consternation spread through Abama, as Araki and his band rode through the hamlet; for the inhabitants, recognising the Emperor's badge embroidered on the surcoats of many of the men, well knew that his emissaries would not travel so far unless they were sent on some very particular duty; and though they for the present left the villagers unmolested, their fears were not allayed by perceiving that they took the private road to the residence of Sako Miyako. As they drew nearer to the house Araki could scarcely restrain his impatience; but his anxieties were somewhat removed, when, on looking around, he could perceive no signs of desertion about the place.

It is not so very long since the Daimio, weary and wounded, found shelter within those hospitable gates, and now does he feel no pang of remorse as he comes an unbidden guest at the head of an armed force! True, he does not intend personal injury to those who then befriended him; he has given the strictest orders to his men to that effect; but still, even his conscience feels a qualm, for he knows that his intentions, if not murderous, are at least very far from righteous. The steward, who has been left in charge of the place, is soon told of the arrival of the strangers; yet not he nor any of the servants dare venture to open the doors. At length, impatient of delay, Araki dismounts and enters the house; rapidly he passes from room to room, even until he reaches that in which he first saw the vision that changed the whole current of his life; but, as he hastily draws back the sliding partition, only a blank, bare chamber meets his view. The room is no longer littered with costly feminine knick-knacks, the sound of music and laughter are no longer heard, and no fair female forms lounge on the long soft mats; the cages of the singing-birds are silent and empty, and the flowers in the window droop their heads, as if grieving for the absence of those by whom they were wont to be tended. Is he indeed too late? has she already gone? Distracted by the thought, which as yet he can scarcely realize, the Daimio rushes through the window into the garden; but there too, all is lonely and deserted; not a human being is to be seen. Then grief and disappointment turn to fury; he stamps with impotent rage, and seeing two beautiful doves tamely pecking beside him, he wrings the neck of one which he knows was Ama's pet, and casting the dead thing from him, unheeding the wailing cry of its mate, he returns to his men, whose countenances indicate that they have been kept waiting quite long enough to try their patience. Now he no longer restrains their desire for mischief; on the contrary with savage energy he tells them that the Christians they sought have already escaped, and he urges them in the Emperor's name to work their will on everything that once was theirs. The fierce band need no second telling; but with yells of approbation they spring from their horses, and, allowing them to wander in the court-yard, they enter the deserted house. To the kitchens they rush in frantic delight, and from the good stock of provisions that they find there it is quite plain that the house has not been long untenanted. The Yakonins and soldiers are hungry and thirsty; their early ride has whetted their appetites, and they eagerly demolish whatever food they find, and drink deep potations of saki, which does not tend to make them more harmless; thus they employ themselves while their leader is wandering through the grounds, vainly seeking for some one to give him information of the family,—vainly indeed, for the steward and other servants have slipped off to the village to warn the inhabitants of their impending danger. Rapidly the news spreads through the valley; the peasant in the fields hastily throws down his implements of labour, and hurries to his home to save his wife and children, by flying with them to the woods; soon the hamlet is almost deserted, only a few remain to comfort the sick and aged, who cannot be moved, but who with pious resignation urge their friends to fly and leave them to whatever fate the Almighty has reserved for them,— nor are they indifferent as to what that fate may be, for they remember their Pastor's teaching; and suffering here from many infirmities, they look forward with holy pleasure to their chance of obtaining the golden crown, and being made one of that glorious band who on earth having shed their blood for the Lamb, are ever nearest to His throne in heaven.

It is well for Orra, the singing-girl, and ex-handmaid of Ama, that she is far out of the way of Araki's anger, for he believes that he owes all his disappointment to her, and he is almost beside himself when he thinks of what might have been had she, according to promise, given timely information of the projected flight. At last, while at the verge of despair, he sees two coolies hurrying across a ricefield near the house; doubtless they belong to Sako, and he orders his men to pursue them, and bring them before him. The terrified creatures run when they see the Yakonins; but Araki, in a commanding voice, calls to them to stop, and no harm shall happen to either of them. Thus assured, they suffer themselves to be taken and brought into the presence of the Daimio, when, falling on their faces, they implore of him to spare their lives. He tells them that they are perfectly safe, if they will give true answers to his questions—"When did their master leave the house, and which road did his party take?" To these queries the coolies find it impossible to reply, for the Padre managed all his patron's affairs with such Jesuitical secrecy, that no one in the neighbourhood knew the exact time of his departure; still less had they any idea as to what road the fugitives were likely to take. Now mendacity is a favourite and besetting sin among the Japanese, and these poor

slaves, seeing that their lives depended upon their
giving some information, did not hesitate because they
could not do so with truth. So when the Daimio,
remembering that Sako had relatives in the neighbourhood of Yosiwara, asked had they gone in that
direction, the coolies eagerly caught the idea; "Yes,
the Sama was right: it was to Yosiwara, or Ka-
nawama, somewhere near Fusi-yama the Matchless;"
then, with perfectly innocent faces, they entered into
every particular of the journey, (all drawn from their
own lively imaginations,) and referred their interested
listener to the Padre for confirmation of the same.
The Padre—ah, true!—until now, in the tumult of
his passions, Araki had almost forgotten his existence;
and there he had been wasting his time, and giving
the Priest ample opportunity of escaping. And had
the Padre profited by the time so afforded?

It so happened that, the day before, he had gone
on his usual missionary round to a neighbouring town,
and, returning to Abama, he was met by a party of
the terrified natives, flying for their lives. These
told him of the arrival of the Tycoon's emissaries,
of their pillaging and destroying everything belonging to Sako Miyako; and, even while they spoke,

as they stood on the head of the hill overlooking the valley, a column of white smoke and bursts of flame, announced the fact that the marauding foe had finished their work by setting fire to Sako's beautiful home. For a few moments, the Padre stood gazing on the progress of the fire, which, spreading itself to the surrounding avenue and plantation, would soon reach his own little hermitage near the church. It was a fearful sight; clouds of birds fled from the burning trees, and flocks of water-fowl rose from the ponds with wild screams of terror, swooping in the air as they sought a refuge from the devouring flames; only the stork, true to her maternal instincts, refused to leave her nest, still cherishing her helpless young while the fire rose up around them. Even as a brave sea-captain gazes on the burning of the ship that he cannot save, so the Padre José watched the progress of that destructive fire. It was a hot summer day, there had been no rain for many weeks, the sun had just passed its meridian height, and the trees and shrubs warmed by its noonday glow, burned with terrible rapidity; gradually the consuming flames swept along the hedgerow in the lane, and as they neared the church, the Padre turned away heart-

sick, and, in accordance with the wishes of his terrified
companions, he hurried with them from the distressing scene, and, plunging into the dark forest
that crowned the hills, they wandered through its
mazy labyrinths, eagerly seeking some cave or rocky
den, where they might hide from the fury of their
foes. They were a pitiable group, men, women, and
children, all equally helpless, without any means of
defending themselves, if attacked by the well-armed
Samourai. The Padre found it difficult to sustain the
hearts of his followers, in those days of danger and
distress, for their bodies, sinking from hunger and
fatigue, increased the depressing fears that harassed
their minds, as many of them had to weep over the
uncertain fate of their relatives, and mourn over those
who, through age or infirmity, had been left behind
in the devoted village—and in that village how were
events progressing under the hands of the pagan crew?
Having completed the destruction of Sako Miyako's
mansion, the Samourai, with fiendish cries, rushed on
to the church. As usual, their first wrath was directed
against the cross, which was ruthlessly torn from its
place, and seizing on the vessels of gold and silver,
they set fire to the wood-work and drapery, and,

I

shouting with hellish glee, as they saw the Christian place of worship wrapped in flames, they carried the Christian emblem into the town, and having laid it in the most open space they could find, they called upon the inhabitants to come from their homes and show their attachment to the faith of their ancestors, by trampling under foot the cross of Christ.* A few weak-hearted ones answered the summons, and obeyed the impious mandate; but the Samourai, finding that no more came, broke into the houses, dragged forth the helpless inmates, all of whom refusing to touch the cross with their feet, had their heads chopped off on the spot. Then, not content with destroying the dwellings of the martyrs, they set fire to the still green paddy-fields, and burned the corn that was ripe for the harvest.

Indeed it would be tedious to relate all the atrocities perpetrated by that lawless band, who even slaughtered the hogs† that they found feeding near

* We take a story-teller's licence in this part of our tale, for the ceremony of "trampling on the cross," in strict accordance with history, was not introduced into Japan until the persecution which raged in the year 1636, in the reign of the cruel, vicious Tycoon Yeze Mitsou.

† The Japanese kill hogs for food, but have a great horror of slaughtering either cows or bulls. They never eat the latter, giving

the cottages; the cows, with their young calves; the quiet oxen that stood in the fields, still harnessed to the ploughs which had been suddenly deserted by the panic-stricken labouring men. Even Araki was terrified at their mad excesses, for in destroying a whole village, and devastating the neighbouring country, they had far exceeded the Emperor's orders; but he who could not control his own spirit now lost all control over his men; for the wretches, wild with saki, and further intoxicated by the gory streams through which they had waded, would not leave Abama until they had completed their work of desolation; and the sun was sinking behind the hills before he could bring them to anything like order, or induce them to continue their march towards Yosiwara, the object of which was (he said) to search for the Christian priest, who had, in all probability, followed his patron's supposed route to that place.

as a reason that "cows do their duty; they bear calves, they give milk; it is sinful to take the milk, for they require it to rear their calves, and because they do this they are not allowed to work. The bulls do their work; they labour at the plough, they get thin, you cannot eat them, it is not just to kill a beast that does its duty; but the hogs are indolent, lazy, do no work; *they* are proper for food."— See *Beecher's Voyage of H.M.S. Samarang.*

The Christian priest; aye, that was a game worth seeking; and with this fresh object to re-stimulate their movements, the savages at last consented to obey their leader, while their hellish shouts and wild yells of triumph startled the evening hour, as they rode from the hitherto peaceful and happy, but now bleeding and desolate Vale of Abama.

CHAPTER XIII.

———

"Trembling, they start, and glance behind
  At every common forest sound,
The whisp'ring leaves, the moaning wind,
  The dead leaves falling to the ground;
As on with stealthy steps they go,
Each thicket seems to hide a foe."

BUT all this time, how has it fared with the party on their way to the sea coast? No obstacle occurring to impede their progress they vigorously pursued their journey, and having put up an ample store of provisions there was no need for them to enter any of the villages that dotted the country through which they passed; so avoiding the high road they chose the unfrequented mountain paths, resting at night

in the most sheltered spots; Sako, his daughter, and
her handmaidens sleeping in their norimons, the armed
men, coolies, and luggage bearers lying around them,
with no better beds than the mossy banks, and the
blue canopy of heaven to serve as a curtain. From
the time that they parted from the Padre, Ama's
heart sank within her, and she began to feel some
of that indescribable loneliness and depression, only
known by those who have been forced to leave a
happy home to wander homeless through a cheerless
world. But you will say, Ama, though homeless
was not friendless, she had her father to cheer and
direct her. But, alas! that father, sadly changed by
recent events, was utterly incapable of any mental
exertion, allowing himself to be borne along in his
norimon, either smoking his faculties into a dreamy
state of stupor, or weeping like a child at being
thus forced to encounter a perilous journey in his
old age. Poor old Sako! his Christian faith was not
of the strongest, he had still a hankering after the
old regime; and but for his daughter he would
gladly have remained at Abama, and returned to the
service of his heathen gods.

So long as the weather was propitious the travel-

lers made rapid progress; but one night having
halted at the edge of a broad belt of forest land, their
slumbers were suddenly broken by a sound, like the
rumbling of distant thunder; yet it was not thunder
that disturbed the midnight air, it was the voice of
the dread typhoon, roaring through the trees of the
forest, every one of which in the agony of its tempest
throes, creaked and groaned, as if endeavouring to
resist the giant foe that was tearing it from its roots.
The great branches bent and swayed with the storm,
threatening every moment to fall with destructive force
on the heads of the encamped party, who lay crouched
to the earth, as the hurricane swept over their heads.
This storm of wind was followed by a deluge of rain,
from which their umbrellas, and cloaks of oil-paper
or split reeds,* could scarcely afford the needful protection; altogether, the travellers were right glad when
the perils of that night were over, and the sun again
arose to cheer them on their way; and sorely they
needed cheering, for the mountain paths had been

* The garments of split reeds worn by many of the Japanese,
form rather unsightly, but perfectly waterproof cloaks; they are
much used by the Yakouins when on active service, during the
rainy season.—See *Alcock's Capital of the Tycoon.*

changed to rivers of mud, and the swollen streams
had overflown their banks, reducing the low country
to a state of swamp. Yet Ama, fatigued in body
and anxious in mind, never allowed herself to appear
fearful; but, timid as she was by nature, enduring
Christian faith gave her strength to meet every
emergency, and it was to her that all the party
looked for direction and comfort, while on her devolved
the task of urging on the men, cheering her handmaids, and soothing her aged father. At length
they descended the last remaining hill, and reached
a wide branch of the river, at whose mouth Yoriama's ship lay at anchor. But here a fresh diffi-
culty awaited them, for the flood was so high that
the fording place was invisible, and the torrent
swept on with a force that seemed to render any
attempt at crossing utterly impracticable. The porters too, whose business it was to carry passengers over
the ford, were nowhere to be seen; then at last Ama's
courage threatened to give way, and as she saw a
column of horsemen riding at rapid pace along the
Tocado,* she wrung her hands in an agony lest here
at the last moment they should fall into the hands

* Tocado or Tokado—the government high road.

of the dark Daimio of Hakoni. But though her earthly parent was powerless to counsel or protect, her Almighty Father was still mindful of her, and she had scarcely uttered a hurried prayer for Divine aid, ere assistance appeared, for the porters came running to the spot, and though they shook their heads when they saw the state of the river, a promise of double pay stimulated their energies, and while even at the ford the water rose above the middle of their bodies, they struggled bravely on, fearlessly doing battle with the surging element, as linked together in one long human chain they succeeded in picking their way safely, and soon deposited their anxious burdens on the opposite side of the river.

At this point all the perils of their land journey were happily ended, for there they were met by Yoriama, who had long been anxiously expecting their arrival, and who had everything arranged for their immediate embarkation on board his strong, well-built ship ; but now a new delay occurred, and perhaps our inland readers may, in some measure, sympathise with the old Japanese gentleman, who during all his life had never beheld the salt sea waves, except as he saw them in the distance from his own native hills.   At first he could scarcely be persuaded to enter the long sharply-built boat, that was to bear him to the ship, and even when safely placed beneath the light housing by which one half of it was protected, he cowered down, silent and trembling, while the boat shot swiftly over the waters.   Ama, though somewhat awed, was not frightened at the novel scene around her, and even her timid handmaids forgot to be nervous, as they gazed with admiring wonder into the clear deep water, teeming with all the glories of marine animal and vegetable life, or raised their eyes to the high cliffs that loomed darkly as they dashed past them, startling many a wild sea-bird from its perch on the craggy height.   As Ama's foot stepped lightly on the deck of the outward-bound ship, a weight of anxious care seemed to be lifted from her heart; involuntarily her thoughts arose in thanksgiving to Him who had preserved her and hers through a host of perils and dangers; and if the young girl's eyes were by and bye dimmed with tears, as they bade adieu to her fair native land, those tears were not shed for herself, but for the memory of that good, that beloved friend whom she had so unwillingly left behind.

CHAPTER XIV.

———

"The baby wept—
The mother took it from its nurse's arms,
And soothed, and hushed its vain alarms;
And baby slept.

"The baby weeps again;
And God doth take it from its mother's arms,
From present pain and future unknown harms:
And baby sleeps."

DR. HINDS.

FOR days the Padre José and his little wandering flock wandered about—wandered they knew not whither; over rocky steppes, and through pathless wild woods, dependent for food on whatever wild fruits or roots, they could find, and sheltering in holes and caves of the earth, where the voice of prayer and praise was often heard; for the men bore their privations patiently; even the weak women scarcely repined, only the little children, deprived of their usual food and shelter, and unskilled in power of self-control, sometimes rent the air, and their parents' hearts, by their piteous wailing cries. Poor infants, He who feedeth the ravens heard them, and many a wailing babe was "taken from its mother's arms, from present pain and future unknown harms;" for the angel hovering over that weary group hushed their feeble cries; and, passing, left many a little one— asleep. One night, being almost perishing with hunger, a council was held, to determine what they must do to obtain food; the Padre said, "Let us trust ourselves in the hands of God, rather than fall into the hands of men;" but from this some of the party dissenting, two of them volunteered to go back to the brow of the hill overlooking the Vale of Abama, hoping that if the foe had left the place they might venture to return to their homes. They went—but sad were their countenances when they returned, for only a few charred posts told the spot where the village once flourished, while the surrounding fields showed, by their blackened appearance, that they too had felt the influence of the devouring flame. No signs of human life were to be seen in the once busy vale;

only a few starving dogs wandered about, howling like wolves that sought for prey. Then the Christians of Abama bowed their heads, and wept over the memory of their happy homes; and though they followed their pastor's voice, and blessed His name who had given, and also taken away, they all felt that they had no resting place, but were henceforth "strangers and pilgrims on the earth." The next day, travelling on, they suddenly came to an opening in the wood that brought them out on a rough high road leading to the town of Tai. On ordinary occasions Tai would have been a safe retreat for the travellers, for there were Christians there who were known to the Padre, but this being the day of the "Matsuri" (or feast) many strangers were passing that way. There were refreshment sheds at intervals on the road, and the party eagerly hurried to the nearest of them, where their pastor purchased food for himself and his followers. The accommodations and eatables at this stall were of the humblest and coarsest description; but famishing men are not particular, and the half blind O-i-tarfi-to,* who kept it,

* Old man.

while serving his customers, was unable to perceive that one among them was a foreigner. Had he been aware of that circumstance he would not have dared to give them a morsel of food, not even a cup of cold water; for only a day or two before, the Tycoon's troops had passed through the town, and warned the inhabitants, at the peril of their lives, to give food or shelter to any foreigners, or strangers suspected of being Christians.

As I said before, it was a festive day at Tai; and although the hour was still early the place was thronged with people of all sorts: strolling musicians, professional mendicants, jugglers, itinerant merchants, vendors of cooked fish and luscious sweetmeats, all forming a Babel of confusing sounds; while here and there a solitary individual claimed public attention, by elbowing his way through the crowd, and holding up little square boxes, and pocketing small pieces of money from those who were willing to part with their " itziboos," for the pleasure of possessing private peep-shows, for by placing the eye to the tiny hole at each side of the little box the spectator would be gratified by a sight of the interior of a Daimio's mansion, with four different suites of apartments. Such

are the delights of the noisy natives; noisy in the
noon-day, but much more so at night, when the
quieter folks having gone to their homes the spirit
of merchandize departs, and only the demon of
saki reigns supreme; then he who before carried
about his wares, suffers himself to be half carried
home by his connubial partner, who, lantern in
hand,* supports her helpless spouse, giving him
many a cuff and hearty shake, but ultimately saving
him from falling a victim to the drunken mirth of
the savage two-sworded bullies, who walk about in
troops, attacking and challenging after the manner
of those roystering bands who at the other side of
the globe, even in civilized Britain, were wont to
disturb the midnight quiet in the streets of London
and Edinburgh—for in all ages and in all climes, be
the agent saki or alcohol, the effects are still the same,
effacing the Divine image, and causing human beings

---

* Lanterns are much used by all classes in Japan; indeed, no
person is allowed to move on land or water without one; officers and
people of rank, when making their visits of ceremony by day, are
always preceded by their lantern-bearer. These lanterns are of
various forms, and composed of various substances; sometimes of
paper, painted with different devices, and sometimes of a pellucid
horny substance, made from the gum of the "Agal, Agal," which
is not a bad substitute for glass.

to cease to be human, by placing them on a level with the beasts that perish. But to return to the Padre. Having placed the women and weaker members of his flock in a safe asylum, with friends who were able and willing to shelter their suffering fellow-Christians, he blessed them, and went on his way, accompanied by a faithful few who would not be parted from him. He had procured a Japanese dress, which he put on over his priestly garments, and with his head enveloped in a huge straw hat, he thought he might safely pass through the busy crowd. But, however disguised in dress, he could not alter the cast of his features, and his hat getting pushed aside, as he forced his way through the throng, his foreign countenance attracted the notice of some Yobos* who were attached to a party of pilgrims then halting at Tai, on their road to the "Holy Mountain." These having travelled by way of Abama had learned with satisfaction of the destruction of that flourishing Christian church; they knew that the government authorities were seeking the Christian priest; and no sooner had the Padre

---

* Martial priests.

José's European features caught their eye than they raised a hue and cry after him; he was immediately surrounded, and dragged before the Atono of Tai,* who decreed that he was to be forthwith driven from the town. The Yoboos were much disappointed at the leniency of this sentence; they had long been irritated at the progress of a religion that had deprived the gods of Japan of thousands of worshippers; and now that they had a Christian priest and Christian converts in their hands they would not let them off so easily. They knew that the emissaries of the Tycoon were before them on the road, and they hoped for a rich reward from their leader, if they delivered the Christians into his custody. So the Padre and his friends found themselves in the midst of a band of heathen fanatics, inveterate enemies of the Cross, who delighted in reviling at the Christian religion, and uttering† blasphemous threats of vengeance on the Christian's God.

* Mayor of the town.

† In the year 1640, when four of the principal citizens of Macao were sent to remonstrate with the Japanese Government for their rigorous proceedings against the Christians and foreigners, they were seized and immediately put to death for having presumed to enter Japan, when they were aware of the edict which had been passed

K

On reaching Yosiwara the heathen pilgrims perceived a number of two-sworded men lounging about the principal honjen in the place ; these were, in fact, some of Araki's party, and the great Daimio himself was even then in the house, boiling with rage at having been baffled in his search for Sako Miyako and his daughter. No sooner had his men announced that the yoboos had taken a foreign priest than, in breathless haste and forgetful of dignity, he threw down his pipe and hurried to the door, where he had no sooner shown his awful presence than all the assembled priests and pilgrims fell on their faces before him ; only one tall form remained erect ; not even to the Imperial Pontiff would he now make a reverence that was refused by the angel in Holy Writ, much less would he bow himself down to a proud Pagan prince ; yet, with all the courtesy of his nation, he acknowledged the great man's rank ; but not in a manner to satisfy Araki, who scowled at the priest

prohibiting all foreigners from landing on Japanese shores. The following impious inscription was put on their grave :—"So long as the sun shall warm the earth let no Christian be so bold as to enter Japan, and let all know that the king of Spain himself, or the Christian's God, or the Great Saka will, if he violate this command, pay for it with his head."—See *Beecher's Voyage of the Samarang.*

for daring to remain standing in his presence. He
might have forced him into submission, but there
was a calm firmness in the Padre's eye that promised
no easy conquest, and just now he did not choose to
resort to any severe measures. He had sought everywhere for Ama and her father—had sent scouts into
all the neighbouring towns, but with no success;
such a party of travellers could not have passed
unnoticed, and they had not been seen by any one.
It was plain that the coolies must have deceived
him in order to obtain their own release; but the
Padre was better informed, and by fair means, or
foul, he should be forced to confess all he knew. But
the old proverb says, "we may take a horse to the
water, but we cannot make him drink," and so, though
Araki had caught the Padre, he could not force him
to speak, and though he underwent a rigid examination in the Daimio's private room, he would give no
information as to his patrons' movement that could
serve as a clue to their pursuers. Araki was wholly
unprepared for such obstinate resistance to his wishes,
and, stranded as he was in his dearest hopes, he
would not yet give up, but determined to pursue
the matter to the utmost. The Pagan priests were

clamorous for the Christians to be forced to accompany them to the end of their pilgrimage, alleging that it would give those who might recant, time to do so, while those who still remained true to the Cross should be given to appease the wrath of the Great Dragon, or, in other words, to be thrown into the crater of the Holy Mountain.*

So far as the Padre was concerned, Araki felt inclined to demur against their request; the Daimio was not influenced by religious zeal in his perse- cution of the Christians; it was entirely to carry out his own designs, and though he disliked Christianity, his dislike was wholly on political grounds, for, as far as religion itself was concerned, he had the contempt common to many of his princely order, most of whom were "Taouists" or Sceptics, caring very little for any form of faith, regarding them all as varied species of priestly humbug. On any ordinary occasion he would not have demeaned himself by accompanying a set of enthusiasts belonging to a

---

* During the persecutions of the seventeenth century, the boiling crater of Mount Ungen, or Ungu, was made a common instrument of death to the Christians, numbers of whom thus suffered from the relentless fury of their Pagan adversaries.

class so far beneath him in social position, but now he hoped that, by harassing the Padre with a heavy pilgrimage, his enfeebled bodily strength would so weaken the powers of his mind that when the last terrible moment was come he would be willing to divulge all he knew; so, to the amazement of all, (who had never before heard of a Daimio undertaking the great pilgrimage,) he ordered his followers to place themselves at the head of the party bound for Fusi-yama, and, for greater expedition in travelling, the Padre was obliged to mount a wild, unbroken horse, which could not have been managed by any one less skilled in horsemanship than he was, for in the olden time, before he took the priestly vows, Don José de Sebina was one of the most accomplished cavaliers that graced the court of Lisbon.

After a long ride through an open country, rich in expansive fields of rice and corn, they came to a wild district, where the land, no longer fit for cultivation, was covered with long rank grass; passing this they entered a thick wood that clothes the base of the "Holy Mountain," where their unexpected presence caused no small amount of consternation among a herd of deer which, turning startled glances on the

intruders, trotted off with that nimble grace so peculiar
to the antlered kings of the forest; now and then
a wild boar crossed their paths, while thousands of
rabbits scampering off became lost in their earthy
homes. On reaching the very centre of the wood the
party halted before a great heathen temple, or monastery, where they purposed to await the arrival of the
other prilgrims who, having paused at various shrines,
and roadside places of rest, were necessarily much
slower in their progress. There was immense excitement in the monastery when it was known that the
great Daimio of Hakoni was about to halt there on
his way to "Fusi-yama the Matchless;" and the high
priest himself came to the door to receive his illustrious
guest, allowing his sacred brow to touch the ground
in token of respect for so great a personage. As
they could not proceed any further on horseback
the horses were put up in a place of shelter, while
the Daimio and his retinue proceeded to enjoy the
hospitalities which the priests set before them. No
one offered anything to the poor Christians or their
priest; and the latter, though little inclined to eat, was
suffering so much from thirst that at last he ventured
to ask for a drink of water. His request was answered

by sneers and insults, but a soldier, more merciful than the rest, tossed him a bunch of half-ripe grapes. At another time he might have rejected the un-promising fruit, but now they were pleasant to his parched mouth, while their sour flavour refreshed his sinking soul, for it reminded him of the vinegar offered by other Pagan soldiers to the great God-man; his heart was lifted up within him, and he gloried in the thought that he, the sin-stained follower, should be counted worthy to receive similar treatment to his sinless Lord.

The Pagans having refreshed themselves to their satisfaction, threw the remainder of their repast to the half-famishing Christians; not from any feelings of compassion for the sufferings of their fellow-mortals, but from a fear that, if not fed, they would never be able to accomplish the journey before them, and perhaps might even fall down and die by the way, and so cheat the disciples of the Sintoo faith out of the acceptable sacrifice which they hoped to offer to the Great Spirit of the Mountain. As the pilgrim party were very numerous, of course the Temple could not accommodate them all; and while the best part of the place was given up to the

Daimio and his personal attendants, and the next best was placed at the service of the travelling priests and pilgrims, the poor Christians were thrust into a stable with the hogs and cattle, around which an armed band of soldiers and Yakonins kept watchful ward during the hours of darkness. Yet truly these gave themselves needless trouble; for no thought of escape ever entered the mind of any one individual in that little Christian company, who (though they would willingly have kept vigil with their beloved pastor) one by one dropped off into a deep and tranquil sleep, while to the Padre (weary in the flesh, but his mind at peace with God) it was also given to enjoy one brief but peaceful slumber ere the first glimmer of that morning dawn, which was to him "the eve of death."

CHAPTER XV.

NEVER had the Eastern sun, rising in glory over
the isles of Japan, shed its lovely beams on a more
incongruous party than that which left the court-
yard of Onio, in marching order, for their arduous
up-hill journey. First, there were the Yamooshees
(or men of the mountain), to act as guides, by
showing the easiest and safest path up the steep
ascent; then came the Daimio's men, and their pri-

soner, followed by the other Christians, strictly
guarded by a band of vengeful Yoboos; while the
heathen pilgrims, and the Bonzes, carrying the sacred
emblems, and chanting sacred songs, closed the procession. For hours and hours they toiled along the
steep ascent, up a stony path, often broken by sharp
rocks, and piles of rough loose scoriæ; the heathen
enthusiasts quietly enduring the fatigues that were
to bring them immunity from every human ill, and
their priests exulting in the horrors about to be
done, and the sacrifice about to made to the Spirit *
of their Holy Mountain. But the Daimio—we know
he has no religious fervour to sustain him, nor is he
comforted by any belief in benefit to be derived from
his exertions; and very soon he begins to find out
that he has imposed a very severe penance on himself; yet his bull-dog tenacity does not suffer him to
yield; on the contrary, he is determined to endure
anything, rather than let go his hold of the last

---

* Pilgrimages to the Holy Mountain are made in honour of the
founder of the Sintoo religion, who for some time took up his abode
on Fusi-yama. The Sintoo is the oldest of the Japanese sects, and
the spirit of its founder is still supposed to hover about the Holy
Mountain, giving health and every other blessing to those who
perform the pilgrimage from respect to his memory.

remaining chance of securing the prize for which he has so long plotted and schemed. His temper is not improved by his sufferings, and he gives vent to it in loud execrations at his men, who, in their turn, curse him in their hearts, and openly revile the Padre, for causing them all this unnecessary fatigue. Now and then the party halt for breath, and then only one of their number, unheeding fatigue and the bitter cold of the rarefied atmosphere, has eyes to see, and a heart to enjoy, the beauty of the glorious view around him. Rich valleys, and broad cultivated plains; the long mountain range, with a blue lake calmly nestling in its bosom; the dark woods, where broken lines of silver show the course of many a mountain torrent; and, far away, the broad waters of the great Pacific dancing in the sunshine, as the long waves ebb in and out of the narrow creeks, and open harbours that line the rugged coast. Still on the pilgrims go, still upwards, higher and higher, while the clouds roll beneath them, and the cold becomes so intense, that the natives are fain to cover up their ears and noses, to protect them from its nipping influence. But the Padre feels no cold, or, if his mortal coil suffers, his soul perceives it not, for the Holy Spirit has shed its warming rays into his heart, and he thinks he sees his Father's face beaming with approving smiles from the blue arch above him. He loves earth's glowing landscape, that is stretched in beauty round him, yet he heaves no sigh as he turns from it, and continues his up-hill journey, every step of which is bringing him nearer and nearer to the golden plains of heaven. Repeatedly has Araki appealed to him to answer his questions, and as repeatedly have the Pagan priests besought him to curse his God, and save his life; but, did he not refuse them when in the world below, and still within reach of earthly ties, and now that all earthly influences have faded from him, and earthly life has almost passed away, will he *now* deny his Saviour? Nay, " to whom much is forgiven, the same loveth much ;" and instead of cursing his God and denying the faith, with all the energies of his soul his voice breaks forth in praise, as he chants the " Hallelujah Chorus," which, being caught up by his Christian brethren, swells out into a heavenly strain, sounding still louder in the calm, clear mountain air, while the hills send back an echo of the blessed sounds, and the Pagans, terrified at hearing them repeated afar off, fall on their faces in fear and trembling, thus doing involuntary homage to the Great King of Heaven.

Fusi-yama* was not then, as now, an extinct volcano; and though years had elapsed since any eruption had taken place, the mountain constantly emitted smoke and lava, while subterranean sounds indicated continued subterranean activity. So it was that, as the last echoes of the "Hallelujah" had died away, and while the Pagans were still paralysed with fear, a low rumbling was heard deep down in the bowels of the earth. At this the priests start up. "The Great Dragon is angry," say they, "and the Spirit of the Mountain calls for the blood of the Christian devils. Come on! come on! Can the Great Saka help them now? Their God has spoken, but he comes not: come on, lest the dsi-sin-nai comes to swallow us up." Thus urged, the pilgrims hurry on, and soon reach the summit of the mountain. Before leaving Onio, a heavy cross of wood had been laid on the shoulders of the Christian priest, who, more than once, must have sunk under its weight, but for the assistance of

* The last eruption occurred in the year 1717. It was of a very terrific nature, but since then the volcano has ceased to give any indication that a similar event is likely to occur again.

his friends; yet, though flesh succumbed, the spirit
was always strong and willing, so that whenever he
failed, he quickly recovered himself, and went on
glorying in his burden, the sharp pressure of which
sent thrills of pleasure through his sinking frame,
for did not *He*, the Heavenly Martyr, ascend the hill
of Calvary, borne down by the weight of *His* cross?
and, thinking on this, the Padre José felt humbly
grateful that, after all the years of his life spent in
folly and in crime, his forgiving Father should confer
on him the inestimable blessing of dying for the
glory of God, and bearing his beloved banner even
to the very last.   On reaching the summit of the
mountain, the Bonzes and Yoboos again assailed the
Christians with temptations to renounce the Christian
religion; but even the poor natives were strong in
the faith of Christ, and their courage was increased
by the constancy of their beloved Pastor.   Even as
heathens, death had no terrors for them; and now
they looked with more joy than fear on the short,
dark road that was to lead them to eternal bliss.
Not one of them would deny their Saviour, or do
despite to His cross.   Again the rumbling sounds
were heard deep down in the heart of the mountain,

again the Pagan priests called the attention of the
people to these tokens of impatience on the part of
the fiery Dragon, and a volume of smoke at that
moment issuing from the crater, it seemed indeed as
if some great monster was there, puffing and fuming
with suppressed wrath. Without more words, the
unresisting Christians were seized by the frantic
Yoboos, while all the Pagans uttered hellish cries, as
they saw them hurled into the fiery depths below.

By the Daimio's orders the Padre was the last
to undergo the test, and while he was silently pray-
ing for the departing souls, he was interrupted by
Araki, importuning him to tell him where Ama was,
and whatever his religious faith might be his life
should be spared. But the Christian Pastor was
neither a traitor to his friends nor to his God, and
he smiled pityingly at the earnestness of his per-
sistent foe; but that smile was changed to one of
triumph when giving a parting glance to earth his
eye rested for a moment on the ocean, where something like a large white bird floated from the mouth
of a little rock-bound harbour. The Padre knew
what harbour that was, and as the sun shone
brightly over the floating speck the white sails of a

ship were distinctly visible; a ship, a large ship too, and the good priest's heart beat gladly, for now he knew that his earthly troubles were indeed ended, and Ama, his precious lamb, was safe from the toils of the heathen wolf. With joy he raised his eyes to heaven, and—"My Father, I thank Thee—my Saviour I adore Thee," broke from his grateful lips. The words were in Japanese, and he was murmuring others in his own soft native tongue, when the Daimio, who had followed the direction of his eye when gazing on the ocean, seemed now to comprehend the truth, and pointing to the outward-bound ship, "Ama! there," he exclaimed, and waited breathless to have his fears confirmed. "Even so," was the calm reply, and the Christian Pastor meekly bowed his head, then twining his arms more firmly round his cross, he raised his eyes to heaven; perhaps he there saw visions of a host encamped around him, for he continued gazing upwards with a stedfast smiling face, whilst his enemies rushed upon him with fiendish shouts, and finding it impossible to sever him from the emblem of his faith they lifted him and it high above the yawning crater, and flung him into the deep abyss below. And the Daimio:

disappointed in all his hopes, he turned his flaming eyes from the Martyr's grave to the shining waters of the Pacific: there they were dancing in the sunshine, and seeming to mock his impotent grief and wrath, while they bore the being he loved for ever from his sight:—while, far away, on the edge of the blue horizon, a tiny speck showed all that was now visible of the outward-bound barque. Soon that too was gone, and with it the last remaining ray of hope faded from the Daimio's mind, leaving nothing to supply its place but a chaos of rage and blank despair. When Araki was angry, he was like one possessed; and (like all ungovernable furies) he always wreaked his vengeance on whoever or whatever came nearest to his hand. We have seen him on a former occasion venting his angry disappointment on an in-offensive bird, and now he turned his wrath on the hapless, and almost as helpless Pagan pilgrims; for some of them, interfering to protect a priest whom he chose to insult, were immediately knocked down by the fierce Samourai. Thus the God of the Christians avenged Himself on the murderers of His people, while the very heavens themselves seemed to participate in the wrath of their King. The sky

L

became suddenly overcast; the thunder rolled and reverberated among the mountains; the blue, laughing waters of the ocean were changed to a hue of dusky green; and wreaths of white foam crested the angry looking waves. Meanwhile a conflict was raging on the "Holy Mountain," where Pagan swords were turned upon each other; and on that fatal day the volcanic soil of "Fusi-yama the Matchless" drank in other blood than that of the Christian martyrs.

CHAPTER XVI.

> . . . . "To die, to sleep;
> No more; and by a sleep to say we end
> The heart-ache, and a thousand natural shocks
> That flesh is heir to; 'tis a consummation
> Devoutly to be wished! To die, to sleep!"
>
> SHAKESPEARE'S *Hamlet.*

WHILE Araki the Daimio was away nominally on the Tycoon's business, but in reality for the benefit of his own devices, his enemies at Yeddo were not slow in taking advantage of his prolonged absence. As time passed, the Emperor began to wonder what delayed him so long, and from every courier that came in from the provinces he looked for some account of his proceedings; but time went on, and the minister neither returned to court, nor sent any account of himself to his expectant monarch, who began to chafe at the apparent neglect of his favourite. Then it was that the Prince of Yicko (of whose harem Orra, the singing girl, was now the reigning queen) began to creep into the royal confidence, and in doing so, contrived to drop many a well-timed hint as to the true nature of Araki's motives for proceeding against the Christians of Abama. Added to this, while the iron was hot against him, one of his men returned alone to Yeddo, wearied out with hardship and fatigue, having come across the country, and ridden hard so as to arrive at the capital before the rest of the band. This worthy was indeed the Ometsky (or spy) who had been appointed to follow Araki, even as his shadow, to report all his words and actions, and if possible to divine the very thoughts and motives which actuated all his movements. The Ometsky's account acted like oil on the flame of the Tycoon's wrath against his favourite; he had always entertained a sincere dislike, founded on intense jealousy, of the class to which Araki belonged, though for himself individually he had felt a decided partiality, believing him to be one who would sacrifice all private interests for the cause of his sovereign, and the ancient religion and government of his country. Judge then his surprise and indignation at discovering that *he* had actually been made use of as a tool to further the private feelings of one of the proudest of his proud feudal lords. Those who esteem themselves wiser than their fellow-men are especially annoyed when they find they have been duped : to Taiko Sama the idea was truly galling; for while he daily tried to put down his other proud nobles, he had tolerated and confided in Araki, believing that he at least was free from selfish designs, and had undertaken an expedition little congenial to his taste, solely from a regard for his sovereign and a desire to see the people of Japan restored to the religion of their ancestors, instead of being led away by foreigners to serve their God, and perhaps in the end to yield obedience to the secular power of some foreign potentate. Yet, even with·all the evidence against him, Taiko was slow to believe that he had been deceived in his favourite minister; but Araki's enemies, having once applied the wedge, took care to work on so as to widen the breach: and when the Tycoon heard all that Orra had to tell of the Daimio's sudden passion for Ama the Christian, her rejection of his suit, and his determined persistence in it, all his doubts vanished, and the darkest suspicions took possession of his mind; every action of his late favourite was reviewed and weighed, and he was accused of sinister designs that he never really entertained. There was reason in this, too; for Taiko argued that the man who could dare to borrow the Emperor's troops, merely to enable himself to add a new prize to his harem, would not scruple to go to still greater lengths were he to set his eyes on any other object, equally difficult to attain. Orra too, vengeful and depraved as she was, did not scruple to add a great deal of what was *not* true to her true evidence against the man who had scorned and rejected her love; consequently on her testimony, combined with that of the Ometsky, and others who had felt the weight of his tyrannic rule, the Daimio of Hakoni, in heart attached to his sovereign, was accused of plots and intrigues against him; and Taiko Sama in much wrath dispatched a courier to demand his immediate presence in Yeddo, the city of the Tycoons.

CHAPTER XVII

" Farewell ! a long farewell to all my greatness !
  This is the state of man ! to-day he puts forth
  The tender leaves of hope; to-morrow blossoms,
  And bears his blushing honours thick upon him ;
  The third day comes a frost, a killing frost,
  And when he thinks, good easy man, full surely
  His greatness is a ripening, nips his root ;
  And then he falls, as I do."

Soliloquy of Cardinal Wolsey—SHAKESPEARE.

ARAKI, crestfallen and dispirited, was leaving Yosiwara at the head of his men, when they were met by the Imperial messenger; and his heart misgave him as he read the haughty mandate that recalled him to the capital. In the massacre of the native Christians and the destruction of Abama, he knew that he had far exceeded the orders received; nevertheless, he had hoped to impress the Emperor with a belief that zeal

for the political and religious well-being of his country
had there led him beyond the prescribed boundaries. As to the capture and death of the Portuguese
priest, it would be regarded as a meritorious action;
but the massacre of the pilgrims, on the holy soil of
the Holy Mountain!—that was indeed a stumbling-
block: how would *that* be received at court?

It had apparently cost him one of the Tycoon's
soldiers; and Araki, now for the first time missing
the deserter from his troop, concluded that the man
had fallen in the fray, while his leader's mind had
been in too great a state of turmoil and confusion
to permit of his taking much notice of all that was
passing around him.

Had the news of that unfortunate affair already
reached the capital? if'not, it was at least plain that
the Emperor had some other occasion against him,
or he would never have sent such a peremptory
order for his immediate return to Yeddo. Altogether
the Daimio of Hakoni had derived so little comfort
from a retrospective view of his own proceedings,
that, when he continued to brood over his heart disappointment, he began to regard life as now possessing
few charms for him. To live on, "un-loving and un-

loved," to feel that perpetual heart-ache, " that wild impulse," that mad longing after something he had not, and now could never have, was an existence too fearful for him to contemplate ; for the Pagan Daimio, noble and wealthy as he was in worldly position, was a very bankrupt in spirit, having no hope, no ray of light to cheer him in the gloomy loneliness of his future life. When, therefore, the Tycoon's haughty mandate was put into his hand, he was scarcely affected by it as he might have been ; for it was only the last drop wanting to overflow the already brimming cup of his misfortunes : and, as he read it, his dark eyes kindled with a darker light, his brows bent into one hard straight line, his lips were firmly drawn together, while the teeth within were closely set ; for Araki in his own mind was passing judgment on himself, and deciding his future fate. Two apparitions stared him in the face : of one, grim Death, the proud Pagan felt no fear ; for, believing in no future state of bliss or of woe, the mere termination of a now hateful existence had no terror for him ; but from the other demon — pale, shame-faced Disgrace — Araki's soul recoiled in horror. No, *that* he could never encounter ;

on the contrary, he would take care to keep out of its way: so in calm defiance of all supreme power, he ordered the Emperor's Yakonins and soldiers to return to Yeddo under the command of the young officer who brought the royal message; this done, he left them, and accompanied by his own tried retainers, turned off the Tocado into a by-road that led into a very opposite part of the country. The messenger from the Tycoon, taken by surprise at this unexpected move on the part of the Daimio, paused on his march and stared after the retiring troop, uncertain whether he ought to follow and insist on their returning with him to Yeddo. But as he had received no orders to that effect, and had not a sufficient number of men with him to enforce any submission, he concluded that he would be acting with most discretion by pursuing his own way home with all possible haste, and allowing the disgraced Daimio to proceed unmolested to his own hereditary mansion of Hakoni.

CHAPTER XVIII.

"Rest! Rest! Oh give me rest and peace!
The thought of life that ne'er shall cease
Has something in it like despair,
A weight I am too weak to bear.

Sweeter to this afflicted breast
The thought of never ending rest!
Sweeter the undisturbed and deep
Tranquillity of endless sleep!"—LONGFELLOW's *Spanish Student*.

"The undiscovered country, from whose bourn
No traveller returns, puzzles the will,
And makes us rather bear those ills we have
Than fly to others that we know not of."—SHAKESPEARE's *Hamlet*.

IN our first chapter my readers may remember having
seen Araki the Daimio leaving his princely home in
all the pomp of feudal grandeur. Then his mind was
filled with real uneasiness as to the political and
religious condition of his native land; and he was
beginning his journey to Yeddo with the full inten-
tion of exterminating the new creed which he con-
ceived to be likely to acquire a pernicious influence

over the people and government of Japan. With these views he had first stirred up Taiko Sama to take measures against the foreigners and the religion they had so successfully promulgated; but afterwards, when completely under the influence of one dominant passion, political interests and the well-being of his country ceased to be the mainspring of his actions; and though he still continued the farce of zeal for his sovereign, he allowed his public position to become absorbed in his private feelings. Thus the clever politician and wily courtier gradually became a blindly infatuated man, whose whole heart and soul were set on the attainment of one object which, could he have possessed it easily, would soon have become of little value in his eyes. Formerly the hard feudal lord, who never felt for others, would have scouted the idea of his own heart being vulnerable to any tender feelings. A wife was, in his eyes, as any other piece of furniture, to be selected for the adornment of his mansion; and already his money had enabled him to purchase as many as he pleased of those animated playthings whose beauty caught his eye, and of whom he tired as quickly as does a child of his new toys. His feelings for

Ama were of a different nature; she was something more than a painted puppet,* and could she have loved him as he loved, under her benign influence he might have been a better man. I say *might* have, for in such cases the weaker ones do not always succeed; and even when they do, the slender cord that bends the bow is too often worn out by the perpetual effort. At any rate Araki's love met no return; and then thwarted affections, curdling whatever good was in his nature, stirred up his worst passions, set his brain on fire, and so led him on step by step, until he waded through rivers of human blood. Blindly believing that if he could get Ama into his power, he must succeed in obtaining her love, he determined to pursue her to the utmost; but alas! all his efforts recoiled on himself; though he never knew what it was to despair, until his eyes saw the last of those white sails that bore her far from her country and from him. And whose fault was it that she was now for

---

* Many of the Japanese ladies would be very beautiful were it not for the way in which they paint their faces, covering them with a preparation of rice powder that has a very chalky effect, rouging their cheeks, and colouring their lips a bright red. Sir R. Alcock remarks that all these cosmetics give them the appearance of "the figures adorning a Twelfth-night cake."

ever beyond his reach? It was even his own; for had not his machinations driven her from her home in Abama, to seek some quiet spot in a foreign land, where she might dwell secure from persecution, on account of her adherence to the Christian faith? Under all this misery Araki's proud spirit was gradually breaking; and to him the Emperor's mandate was but the finishing stroke to all the misfortunes he had brought upon himself; so his servants at Hakoni had scarcely recovered from their astonishment at his sudden appearance there, ere he issued invitations to his few neighbours to honour him with their company, at an entertainment which he purposed to give at the ancient home of his fathers. A day or two passed—passed heavily enough to Araki the Daimio, who, impatient in all things, longed to urge on the leaden wings of time, every moment of which brought harrowing recollections and miserable thoughts to the now heart-broken noble. Perhaps, like the traitor of old, he felt the curse of God upon him; but if he did, he never recognised from whence it came; he only knew that the earthly monarch whom he had served had turned his face from him, and that he was not only a disappointed, but a disgraced man.

At last the morning of his great entertainment arrived, and, with something akin to joy, he hailed the first gleams of dawning day.

Has there been a fall of snow in the night? or has Araki's mansion been newly whitewashed? Nay, snow does not fall during the summer solstice; and as the soft morning breeze passes over the house, we see that it stirs a snow-white cloth with which the whole exterior is covered. No emblem this of nuptial joy, but rather of deepest mourning; and as the princely owner of the mansion, with many a courteous salaam, receives his most distinguished guests, we perceive that he too is clad in a white robe of hempen cloth, the purity of which is not relieved by any armorial design, or other of the usual embroidered decorations. He looks very pale, but dignified, calm, and solemn, as he walks about among his guests, and partakes with them of the delicate confections and sweetmeats, which, together with saki and other refreshments, are handed round by a train of silent attendants. After this the Daimio, in a low deep voice, addresses complimentary speeches to his friends, who answer softly, and salaam courteously, as he thanks them for the pleasure of their company; indeed, so many smiles

and bows pass between them that we cannot believe
that anything unusual is about to follow. The room
in which the company are assembled is a long spacious
apartment, the walls of which, richly painted, are
now draped in white, while every ornament has been
removed, save the long soft mats, which, as usual'
cover the floor. On these the guests are lounging
or sitting, after the fashion of their nation, enjoying
themselves, with perfect unconcern as to anything
that is to be. At length Araki rises,* and, followed
by his favourite attendant, advances towards that spot
which occupies the chief place of honour in the room.
A solemn silence now reigns among the guests; they
begin to look anxious and expectant. Araki again
turns, and bows a salaam to them all, softly uttering the
word "Saionara;" then they too bow, and give him back
his soft and sad farewell. Again he turns to the mat,
over which he slightly inclines his head, and quickly
drawing his sword,† he gives himself one deep cut

* At this period of the ceremony, if the "Hara-Kiru" (or crucial
incision) be performed by command of his sovereign, the culprit
reads the government order aloud.

† It is deemed an essential point in the education of every
Japanese gentleman that he practise the use of the sword, so as
to be able to perform the crucial incision with equal grace and
dexterity. A second cut is thought a peculiarly brave act.

across the "footo-bara" (or abdomen); then another longitudinal gash up the middle of his body; which done, his faithful attendant (standing behind) chops off his master's head, and a gory corpse is all that now remains of the proud Daimio of Hakoni. The guests silently applaud the deed, and forgetting the faults, they extol the noble qualities of the man who has just terminated his existence by enacting the Hara-Kiru, with a brave dignity well becoming the last of his ancient race. They do not feel as we do, who, only reading the account of such self-destruction, shudder at its ghastly details. Such deliberate suicides are a common every-day occurrence among all classes of people in Japan; they do not even inquire why he has done the deed, suffice it that (according to their notions of etiquette on such an occasion) he has done it well; so they depart in peace to their homes, leaving the Daimio's numerous retainers and servants in a state of anxious uncertainty as to their own future fate: and it is quite probable that, being aware that their master has performed the crucial incision without any order from the government, many of them, dreading the consequences of such an act of bold and open defiance, will not hesitate to follow

M

his example, enacting the Hara-Kiru without the same attendant state and ceremony, but with a stroke quite as effectual as that which terminated the life of the Daimio of Hakoni.

CHAPTER XIX

"Sweet is the smile of home: the mutual look,
  Where hearts are of each other sure;
Sweet all the joys that crowd the household nook,
  The haunt of all affections pure."

KEBLE.

HAVING seen the last of Araki the Daimio, let us leave the " Land of the Rising Sun," and, following the track of a certain white-sailed vessel, speed away to the South, passing the Loo-Choo and Meia-coshima Isles,* and finally landing on Chinese shores; then

---

* Meia-coshima, Mia-cosima, or the Asses Ears, so called because their peaks, when viewed from the sea, have a strange similarity to the long ears of an ass. The natives of these islands are possessed of a remarkable integrity and honesty, both in principle and practice, in which respect they are far superior to their more civilized neighbours of the great island empire.

let us sail into the capacious harbour of Macao, whose
blue waters are shadowed by many a tall-turret
pagoda and imposing fort. As we pass up the
harbour, we notice Chinese and Japanese junks
anchored side by side with the stately galleons of
Western lands, while smaller trading vessels, gondolas,
and innumerable fishing boats, make the waters gay
with busy life. The sun having set does not decrease
the liveliness of the scene, for each vessel is hung
with lanterns; some made of paper of various hues,
others of netted thread, smeared over with "Agal
agal"*—while all combine to produce the dazzling
effect of a general illumination. On landing, we
find the lantern-lit city equally busy; sailors and
mercantile folks hurrying here and there; Portuguese
cavaliers lounging about, smoking, and casting soft
glances at the dark-eyed donnas, who, preserving the
costume of their native land, glide on, (wrapped in

---

* The agal agal is a gum extracted from a marine plant, and is
applied for various purposes, both in China and Japan. The hats of
the Japanese boatmen are sometimes composed of the broad leaves
of the palmetto woven together, and covered with a paste prepared
from the "agal agal." The utility of this pellucid gum is not
confined to the human tribe alone; for the swallows of Borneo
(*Hirundo esculenta*), form their nests of the agal, which nests are
edible.—See *Voyage of the Samarang.*

their graceful mantillas, and attended by their grave duennas,) either to cathedral vespers, or, perhaps, to keep some appointment of which the blind god is the chief instigator. A contrast, they, to the Chinaman, with Tartar countenance and lengthy pig-tail, so gravely plodding on his way, or to the small-footed China-woman, awkwardly hobbling through the crowd. It is a beautiful evening ; and as we leave the city,* and pass along the suburbs, we see mansions built in the European style, the windows opening into long balconies, filled with flowers, and now gaily illuminated with lamps of varied hues. Most of the windows are open ; and, as we pass, we hear many a sweet voice carolling lively songs to the accompaniment of the light guitar. Passing these, we come to a walled-in villa ; but the gates being now closed,

---

* Macao that *was*, and Macao that *is*, are very different places. In the olden time, this grand emporium of Portuguese trade in the East was a wealthy and prosperous city; but from the time that Hong Kong became the seat of British and other European enterprise, Macao, though possessing far greater natural advantages, both as to beauty of situation and salubrity of climate, has gradually fallen into decay. It is no longer a stirring, busy place, but has a miserable, poverty-stricken appearance, its architectural remains speaking sadly of the glories that have been ; while its population, composed of refugees from almost every country under the sun, are a poor and hopeless-looking people.

we cannot hope for entrance to-night, and, as my readers may not wish to wait, I may as well tell them that in this pleasant residence, which so curiously combines Eastern with Western tastes in its arrange- ment, dwells one with whom we have had some recent acquaintance. The house, built in accordance with the Japanese fashion, is a wooden edifice, elegant in struc- ture, and situated in a wide court-yard, enclosed by evergreens and flowering shrubs. There are gardens, too, and grottoes, fish-ponds, and fountains; and, above all, flowers in profusion—flowers everywhere shedding every variety of delicious perfume. Ex- ternally, the house is Japanese; but within, though long soft mats cover the floors, there are chairs and tables, and couches too, some of them elaborately carved, and covered with rich brocade; while among the inlaid cabinets, and porcelain vases, are dispersed exquisite pieces of sculpture, and classic statues in bronze and marble.

And what of the inmates of the mansion?

Daily, when the sun is warm, and ere its rays have become too powerful, a white-haired man, bowed down with the weight of years, wanders about the gardens, attended by some three or four children, who delight in guiding their grandsire's tottering steps, filling his lap, and sometimes decking his hoary head, with flowers. He wears the Japanese costume, but the little ones' dress is more in accordance with the quaint European style of the period. Sometimes, when they become too boisterous in their play, a lady appears among them, and leads away the old man to enjoy a siesta within-doors. He hangs upon her arm, and a round, substantial arm it is; and that, too, is a comely, smiling countenance, which looks lovingly on his. The face has lost its delicate beauty of form, but it has gained in intellect; and we think the dark grey eyes are many degrees more expressive than when we first made their acquaintance. Reader, allow for the lapse of years, and believe that that short, stout matron, with the merry, rosy countenance, is even our friend Ama, while the aged man, who for years has been nothing but an ancient child, is Sako Miyako, formerly the rich owner of half the territory of Abama. And the children—behold them running to meet a tall foreigner, whose high, expansive forehead, and dark, liquid, dreamy eyes, bespeak him to be what he is—a learned man and a poet,* exiled by

* Our readers are probably aware that Camoëns (the great

countrymen who could not appreciate his worth, and now happy in the land of his adoption. On him Ama long ago bestowed her hand, her heart, and all her wealth—her wealth of gold and her wealth of love; and as we see him come forward to meet her, bending his tall figure to kiss her still fair brow, and giving his arm to assist her in supporting her aged father to the house, their children clinging about them, or darting off in chase of a gaily-painted butterfly, surely we believe that they are a happy family, happy as Ama deserves to be, after all she suffered through the machinations of her Pagan lover, Araki, the dark Daimio of Hakoni.

Some time ago, even soon after her marriage, news came from Japan that caused her heart to ache, and

Portuguese poet), when exiled from his country, found a home in the neighbourhood of Macao, where his grave is still an object of interest to European travellers. It is described as being situated in a beautiful garden. The tomb itself is a sort of cave, or rather a stone archway, two great stones standing upright like pillars, and a large block resting upon them, surmounted by a bust of the poet. The grave is shaded over by the feathery branches of splendid trees, while above it stands a charming summer-house. This summer-house is, in many places, quite disfigured by names and foolish inscriptions; but, among them all, the traveller's eye is caught by one short, pathetic line, written by a countryman of the deceased; the words " Luis Camoëns, te adorò," speak volumes of affectionate devotion to the dead poet's memory.—See *Beecher's Voyage of the Samarang.*

many tears to fall from her gentle eyes, as she wept over the fate of her first, and best earthly friend, he who had found her in darkness, and shown her the way to endless light; and so much did her poet-husband sympathise with her grief for such a man, that, among the choicest evergreens in his beautiful demesne, he with his own hands erected, and sculptured a white marble cross, while his ever fertile brain found words wherewith to commemorate the life, and death, of the good Christian Pastor of Abama. The last news from Japan was of a more favourable description. It announced the death of Taiko Sama, also telling that his successor, Yeze-Yason (or Gongin), being friendly to the Christians, had revoked all the edicts against them; foreigners were again allowed to carry on trade in the Japanese ports, and, as that would give a fresh impetus to commerce, it seemed probable that Sako Yoriama would again return to his native land. Whether he did go, or not, we cannot say; we only know that Ama, her father, and her poet-husband, lie buried by the white cross, in the beautiful garden of what always was to them a happy home.

A word more, and we have done.

When the war in the Korea terminated, the vic-

torious army again returned to their native land,
sadly thinned in numbers, but crowned with honour,
and commanded by Tatish, the brave soldier, son of
Sako Miyako.   Henceforth, in acknowledgment of
the services he had rendered to his country, Tatish
became the man whom the Tycoon delighted to
honour, and as if in just retribution for the past,
on him was bestowed the vast territory, and ancient
title of, the Daimio of Hakoni.

CHAPTER XX.

————

"Sit still and hear, those whom proud thoughts do swell,
Those that look pale by loving coin too well;
Whom luxury corrupts——

"Let rules be fixed that may our rage contain,
And punish faults with a proportioned pain;
And do not flay him who deserves alone
A whipping for the fault that he hath done."

CREECH.

My story of the olden time being ended, let us fill
up our remaining pages, by tracing the fortunes of
the Christian religion until its final expulsion from
the "Land of the Rising Sun." From the period of
my tale, until the middle of the seventeenth century,
Christianity underwent many vicissitudes, according to
the various dispositions of the reigning Tycoons; and
so it went on, suffering sundry ups and downs until the

great persecution in the year 1636, when the native
Christians were so cruelly treated, that they flew to
arms, and shut themselves up in the fortified town
of Simbarra, where 38,000 of them bravely held out
against a besieging army of 80,000 men. At that
time the Portuguese, and Spanish, were not the only
foreigners who had found their way into Japan. The
Dutch were there too, carrying on a brisk trade with
the natives, and comporting themselves with a grasping
greediness that characterized all their early commercial dealings; never content unless they enjoyed a
complete monopoly of trade, in whatever country they
established themselves. These Dutch merchants, though
nominally Christians, seem to have had no desire to
propagate, or support the Christian faith, the whole
object of their lives was trade; and with hearts
hardened by the greed of gain, in order to curry
favour with the governing powers of the country,
they actually lent their assistance in the destruction
of the Christians, for the besieging army would
never have subdued the brave defenders of Simbarra,
had not the Dutch director "Kockebecker" gone to
their aid, and with his cannon battered down the
walls of the fated city, whose brave garrison were all

slaughtered, fighting manfully to the very last. The Dutch then chose mammon rather than God; and God did not allow them to go unpunished; for though they for many years enjoyed the free trade that they had purchased with blood, they, in their turn, fell victims to the jealousy of the Japanese government, who, seeing little difference between their creed and that of the Portuguese, compelled them to give up all their religious observances; and surely those early Dutch traders could have had little faith or affection for any religion at all; for they accepted every condition imposed upon them, destroying every memento of their creed, while they ceased to observe the Sabbath, and even erased the dates from their public buildings, because those dates implied an acknowledgment of the Christian era; and thus, slaves to mammon, they were content to remain in a state of slavish obedience to the lords of Firando, buying and selling, and getting gain—worldly gain —for which they had sold their souls. Whether they were more honest in their dealings than their predecessors, we can hardly at this time presume to say; at any rate, they never inspired the Japanese with the same undying hatred that always clung to the names and memories of the Portuguese, and a proof of which was given when the Japanese government refused to allow their subjects to trade with the English, because a Portuguese princess then shared the throne of the King of England. Of course the Eastern monarch would never have learned that fact if the Dutch, jealously fearful of others sharing in the good things for which they had sacrificed so much, had not been careful to inform him of it. By and bye they, and all foreigners were driven from the land, and the government, fearful of any renewal of religious contamination, even prohibited the return of any of their own people who happened then to be visiting other countries. Since the olden time we do not see that the Japanese character has undergone any change; the people, though no longer skilful soldiers, are still a hard-working, industrious race, remarkable for the Spartan simplicity and cleanliness of their dwellings and persons. They are still alive to all their old customs and prejudices; the feudal system still exists in full force, and the Daimios themselves, though all-powerful over their own vassals and retainers, are still under the sway of a cruel despotic government, by whose orders, when a Daimio offends (as in the recent case of the Prince of Nagato) his servants, hundreds of innocent beings—men, women, and children, are executed on his account. Surely we must earnestly hope for some alteration in the religion, and government, of a country possessing so many natural advantages; and as Japan now admits representatives from the principal nations of Europe, as well as America, we trust that instead of being jealous of each other, they may combine together to make such commercial arrangements with the powers that be, that Japan men, seeing the beauty of Christian unity, may gradually become less hostile to the Christian faith; and so when heathenish customs shall have passed away—when the upper classes become educated Christians, as well as intelligent beings, and the peasantry are redeemed from the darkness of heathen ignorance, we shall hear of no more cruel deeds; no more massacres, (official or otherwise;) but peace and prosperity, (such as can only be found in happy Protestant England,) may reign in the "Land of the Rising Sun."

London: Benjamin Pardon, Printer, Paternoster-row.

A

SELECT CATALOGUE

OF

Works published by

Jackson, Walford, & Hodder.

London:

27 PATERNOSTER ROW, E.C.

1865.

Christ and Man; or, God's Answer to our

Chief Questions. By WILLIAM BATHGATE. In crown 8vo., price 5s., cloth.

CONTENTS:—1. Our Chief Questions—2. God's Present Answer to Man's Chief Questions—3. The Person of Christ—4. The Offices of Christ—5. Christ in Relation to Mankind—6. Christ in Relation to the Individual Soul—7. Christ in Relation to the Family—8. Christ in relation to the Market—9. Christ in relation to the State—10. Christ in relation to his own Church—11. Christ in relation to the Spirit of the Age—12. The Truth in Christ attested by its Adaptations and Results.

The Divine Treatment of Sin. By J. Baldwin

BROWN, B.A. In crown 8vo., price 5s., cloth antique, red edges.

" We believe this is Mr. Brown's best book."—*Eclectic Review.*

BY THE SAME AUTHOR.

The Divine Mystery of Peace. In crown 8vo.,

price 3s., cloth antique, red edges.

" Will gratify alike both the thoughtful and the devout."—*The Patriot.*

Thomas Raffles, D.D., LL.D. A Sketch. In

crown 8vo., price 1s., cloth limp.

The Divine Life in Man: Fourteen Discourses.

Second Edition, in crown 8vo., price 7s. 6d., cloth.

The Doctrine of the Divine Fatherhood, in

Relation to the Atonement. In crown 8vo., price 1s. 6d., cloth.

John Leifchild, D.D., his Public Labours,

Private Usefulness, and Personal Characteristics. Founded upon an Autobiography. By J. R. LEIFCHILD, A.M. In 8vo., price 10s. 6d., cloth, with Portrait.

" This is one of the most interesting and admirably executed pieces of religious and ministerial biography we have for a long time seen."—*Eclectic Review.*

Lectures on Theology, Science, and Revelation.

By the late Rev. GEORGE LEGGE, LL.D., of Leicester. With a Memoir, by the Rev. Dr. LEGGE, of Hong Kong. Crown 8vo., 7s. 6d., cloth.

" Full of thought, they are by no means 'dry.' The logic, strong and clear, is vitalised by holy feeling; and often, as in the ten discourses on 'The Theory of the Gospel' and the 'Operation of the Gospel,' the style kindles into a nervous and vivid eloquence."—*The Freeman.*

WORKS BY THE REV. CHARLES STANFORD.

Symbols of Christ. In crown 8vo., price
7s., cloth. Now ready.

Power in Weakness: Memorials of the Rev.
WILLIAM RHODES. Cheap Edition, in fcap 8vo., price 2s.

"This memoir is a solid ingot, small in bulk, but with valid mint-mark, and precious in every grain of it."—*Family Treasury.*

"Mr. Rhodes' life was one of singular trial and affliction, and the remarkable development of mental power which he exhibited in the midst of great physical weakness forms the leading idea of the book."—*Record.*

Central Truths. Cheap Edition, in small
crown 8vo., price 3s. 6d., cloth.

" . . . . A brief and sound view of evangelical truth, in attractive language The style possesses the uncommon charm of being at once rich and clear."—*Record.*

Joseph Alleine: his Companions and Times.
CHEAP ISSUE, Second Thousand, in crown 8vo., price 4s. 6d.

"It is beautifully written. There breathes throughout it the spirit of a Christian and a gentleman, the sanctity and the calmness of a man who has no party objects to serve, and the good taste of a writer who has learned wisdom at the everlasting fountain."—*Christian Spectator.*

Instrumental Strength: Thoughts for Stu-
dents and Pastors. Crown 8vo., price 1s., cloth limp, red edges.

"John Foster could not have produced anything more sage-like in thought, or more beautiful in expression."—*Homilist.*

"Full of wise counsel from beginning to end."—*Weekly Review.*

CHOICE EXTRACTS FROM OLD DIVINES.

Wholesome Words; or, Choice Passages from
Old Authors. Selected and Arranged by J. E. RYLAND, M.A. Fcap. 8vo., elegantly bound in cloth, price 3s. 6d., toned paper.

"For the purpose of meditation before the business of the day has commenced, or for suggesting pious and hallowing thoughts at the close of the day, this little volume will be useful, and, where used, popular also."—*The Churchman.*

"A charming volume for occasional reading."—*Reader.*

The Rise and Progress of Religious Life in
England. By SAMUEL ROWLES PATTISON. In post 8vo., price 7s., cloth.

"This work comprises a rich store of historic information of a very valuable kind."—*Homilist.*

"Mr. Pattison has bestowed much research upon his compilation, and relates in a pleasing manner interesting and important facts, some of which are little known."—*Journal of Sacred Literature.*

The Gospel of Common Sense; or, Mental,

Moral, and Social Science in Harmony with Scriptural Christianity. By ROBERT BROWN, Author of "The Philosophy of Evangelicism," &c. In post 8vo., price 3s. 6d., cloth.

"Three thoughtful papers, which the theological student will do well to read and ponder."—*British Quarterly Review.*

The History of the Transmission of Ancient

Books to Modern Times; together with the Process of Historical Proof. By ISAAC TAYLOR. In post 8vo., price 7s. 6d., cloth, a new Edition, revised and enlarged.

"The book is throughout ingenious and interesting."—*Saturday Review.*

By the same Author,

The World of Mind. An Elementary Book.

In post 8vo., price 7s. 6d., cloth.

"It is nowise inferior to his former works, either in vigour and originality of speculation, or in its terse translucent style."—*Eclectic Review.*

Also, by the same Author,

Considerations on the Pentateuch, addressed

to the Laity. Third Edition, in 8vo., price 2s. 6d., sewed.

Christian Faith : Its Nature, Objects, Causes,

and Effects. By JOHN H. GODWIN. In crown 8vo., 6s., cloth.

"It displays considerable ability and originality, and is worthy of a place by the side of the best treatises on the subject."—*Journal of Sacred Literature.*

Pietas Privata : Prayers and Meditations.

With an Introductory Essay on Prayer, chiefly from the Writings of HANNAH MORE. Thirty-eighth Thousand, 1s. 6d., cloth.

English Nonconformity. By R. Vaughan, D.D.

Second Thousand, in 8vo., price 7s. 6d., cloth.

"—— A volume which merits place in the foremost rank of works illustrating the religious history of the country."—*Athenæum.*

Our Principles ; or, a Church Guide for those

holding or seeking Fellowship in Congregational Churches. By the Rev. G. B. JOHNSON. Second Edition, price 9d., cloth.

Palmer's Protestant Dissenters' Catechism.

With Preface by the late Rev. Dr. PYE SMITH. A New Edition, price 6d., or 40s. per 100.

DR. THOMAS'S COMMENTARY ON MATTHEW.

The Genius of the Gospel: a Homiletical

Commentary on the Gospel of St. Matthew. By DAVID THOMAS, D.D., Editor of the "Homilist." With an Introduction by the Rev. WILLIAM WEBSTER, M.A., Joint Editor of "Webster and Wilkinson's Greek Testament." 8vo., price 15s., cloth, red edges.

"Terse, pointed, and forceful—cannot be thoughtfully read without yielding instruction and profit."—*Watchman.*

"A well-furnished, honest, able, and popular Commentary."—*Christian Spectator.*

By the same Author,

The Crisis of Being: Six Lectures to Young

Men on Religious Decision. Fourth Edition, price 1s. 6d. cloth.

Also, by the same Author,

The Progress of Being: Six Lectures on the

True Progress of Man. Third Edition, enlarged, price 1s. 6d., cloth.

Also,

A Biblical Liturgy for Congregational Churches.

New Edition, in crown 8vo., price 4s. 6d., cloth extra.

First Lines of Christian Theology, in the form

of a Syllabus, prepared for the use of the Students in the Old College, Homerton; with subsequent Additions and Elucidations, by JOHN PYE SMITH, D.D., LL.D., F.R.S., F.G.S. Edited by WILLIAM FARRER, LL.B. Second Edition, 8vo., price 15s., cloth.

"To ministers of the Gospel, and to students preparing for the ministry, this volume is the completest and safest guide in theological study to be found, as far as we know, in any language."—*Eclectic Review.*

The Hebrew Grammar of Gesenius. Trans-

lated without Abridgment. By Professor T. J. CONANT. With a Course of Exercises, and a Hebrew Chrestomathy, by the Translator. Royal 8vo., price 6s. 6d., cloth, New Edition.

WORKS BY THE AUTHOR OF "THOUGHTS ON DEVOTION."

Words of Life's Last Years: containing Chris-

tian Emblems, Metrical Prayers, and Sacred Poems, translated from Foreign Writers. In foolscap 8vo., price 3s., cloth.

The Foreign Sacred Lyre. Metrical Versions

of Religious Poetry, from the German, French, and Italian, together with the Original Pieces. In fcap 8vo., 5s. 6d., cloth extra.

The Christian Harp. A Companion to "The

Foreign Sacred Lyre." In foolscap 8vo., price 5s., cloth antique. red edges.

Modern France, its Journalism, Literature,

and Society. By A. V. KIRWAN, Esq., Barrister-at-Law, and Author of the Article "France," in the "Encyclopædia Britannica." In One Volume, crown 8vo., price 7s., cloth.

"An important exposition of the history of our neighbours, rivals, and allies, by a painstaking and able writer, who shows in every part of his work an intimate knowledge of his subject. The book is full of interest, while its style and manner are most masterly."—*Court Journal.*

Celestial Scenery; or, The Planetary System

Displayed. Illustrating the Perfections of Deity and a Plurality of Worlds. By T. DICK, LL.D. Eleventh Thousand, in crown 8vo., price 5s. 6d., cloth. Carefully revised by the Author, with an Appendix. Illustrated with Engravings, and a Portrait.

"An admirable book to put into the hands of youth and general readers."—*Literary Gazette.*

"This familiar explanation of the most interesting phenomena is well calculated to unfold the wonders of astronomy to those who are unacquainted with the mysteries of that science; while those who have learned its principles will derive pleasure from the speculations on the different aspects of our system, as viewed from the sun and the several planets."—*Athenæum.*

By the same Author,

The Sidereal Heavens; and other Subjects

connected with Astronomy, as illustrative of the Character of the Deity, and of an Infinity of Worlds. With numerous Engravings. Sixth Thousand, in crown 8vo., price 5s. 6d., cloth.

"Another of those delightful books of Dr. Dick."—*Nautical Magazine.*

"A very interesting compilation, made by a practical man, and one which we can have no fear of recommending as a fit sequel to the 'Celestial Scenery' of the same author."—*Church of England Quarterly Review.*

NEGRO EMANCIPATION.

The West Indies: Their Social and Religious

Condition. By EDWARD BEAN UNDERHILL, LL.D., Secretary of the Baptist Missionary Society. In crown 8vo., 8s. 6d., cloth.

"We have no hesitation in saying that it is the most valuable work on the West Indies that has been written the last twenty years."—*Christian Spectator.*

A Comprehensive Chart of Ancient and Modern

Chronology: showing contemporary events from the Creation to the present Era: with a comparative view of the Chronology of the Hebrew and Septuagint Versions of the Bible. Compiled as an Assistant to the Student of History, by J. BATES. Price 7s. 6d., in cloth case.

"It is an elaborate table, and exhibits a good deal of historical information, of the kind required in schools and libraries. It cannot fail to be a useful companion to the reader of history."—*Athenæum.*

"The work is very carefully compiled, and cannot fail to be useful, either for reference, or as a companion to historical reading."—*The Museum.*

"Great care has evidently been taken in the compilation . . . the student will find it very serviceable, and it will interest the general reader."—*English Journal of Education.*

WORKS BY EDWIN HODDER.

I.

Tossed on the Waves : A Story of Young

Life. In crown 8vo., price 6s., cloth.

"Mr. Hodder writes in a pleasant sparkling way, and has the knack of carrying his reader merrily with him to the close of the volume."—*Reader.*

"This is just the sort of story that boys delight to read."—*Athenæum.*

"Mr. Hodder tells a story remarkably well."—*Nonconformist.*

II.

Memories of New Zealand Life. In small

crown 8vo., price 3s. 6d., a Second and Cheaper Edition.

"A very graphic description of colonial society."—*Daily News.*

"Animated and vivacious — frank, simple, religious, and sensible."—*British Quarterly Review.*

"The best account we have met with of the various social phenomena of a new colony."—*Westminster Review.*

III.

The Junior Clerk : a Tale of City Life. With

Preface by W. EDWYN SHIPTON, Secretary of the Young Men's Christian Association. In small crown 8vo., Second and Cheaper Edition, price 2s. 6d., cloth.

"We are heartily pleased to see the Second Edition of this most interesting, truthfully drawn, and profitable story. We again commend it without hesitation or reserve to the young men of our middle classes who have to face the toils and temptations of business life."—*Nonconformist.*

Thornycroft Hall : its Owners and Heirs'

By EMMA JANE WORBORSE. Third Thousand, in crown 8vo.' price 5s., cloth.

"It is the healthiest religious tale that has been published for many a day."—*Patriot.*

The First Week of Time ; or, Scripture in

Harmony with Science. By CHARLES WILLIAMS, Author of "The Seven Ages of England," &c. Crown 8vo., price 5s. cloth.

"A book of modest pretensions, but of real worth."—*British Quarterly Review.*

On Health. What Preserves, What Destroys,

and What Restores it. With Ten Engravings. In Ten Letters to a Non-Medical Friend. By JONAH HORNER, M.D. Third Edition, crown 8vo., cloth limp, price 2s.

"Remarkably fitted to be useful."—*British Standard.*

CONGREGATIONAL PSALMODY.

Congregational Church Music. Psalms and

Hymns for Chanting, Practice-Songs for Classes, &c., &c.
(Weigh-House Series.)

A complete List of the Editions and Bindings of the various works
in this Series will be sent post-free on application to the Publishers.

₊ Congregations supplied on the same terms as the " New Congregational Hymn Book."

"Probably the collection best adapted to present powers is the enlarged edition
of 'Congregational Church Music.' "—*British Quarterly*.

"If any competent precentor or leader of a chapel choir gets hold of it, we are
inclined to think he will not rest till he gets it adopted as the tune-book of the congregation."—*Patriot*.

The Congregational Psalmist : a Companion

to all the New Hymn Books. Edited by the Rev. HENRY ALLON
and H. J. GAUNTLETT, Mus. Doc.

A complete List of the Editions and Bindings of the various works
in this Series will be sent post-free on application to the Publishers.

₊ Congregations supplied on the same terms as the " New
Congregational Hymn Book."

"It has every quality that will attract and please at the first glance, and we are
very glad that an incentive should thus be offered to an examination of its contents,
such as we feel they well deserve and will abundantly repay. On the first appearance
of this work we expressed our admiration of the extensive research and discriminating
judgment which the selection of music evinces, and, above all, for its admirable
fitness for the purpose for which it is designed. A further acquaintance with the
book has more than confirmed our first impressions, while its adoption by many
congregations, and the gratifying results which appear in all cases to attend its use,
afford continually multiplying sanctions for our own opinion."—*Evangelical Mag.*

The New Sunday-School Tune-Book. A Com-

panion to the "New Sunday-School Hymn-Book." Edited by
JAMES SAMPSON, Author of "Sacred Harmonies." Square 16mo.,
price 1s. 6d., boards; 2s., cloth; 2s. 6d., roan, gilt edges.

"The tunes are excellent, both intrinsically and in their adaptation to the hymns
which are placed at the foot of each. The melodies are neither commonplace nor
peculiar, but simple and sweet."—*Nonconformist*.

The New Sunday-School Hymn-Book. Edited

by EDWIN HODDER. New Edition, price 2d., in neat Wrapper;
or 3d. in limp covers. A liberal allowance to Schools.

₊ Those desirous of binding the above with books already in
use, will be supplied with copies in quires at 10s. 6d. per 100 net.

PUBLICATIONS OF THE

Congregational Union of England and Wales.

The New Congregational Hymn Book, and
The (Old) Congregational Hymn Book. A

complete List of Sizes, Prices, and Types, with terms to Congregations, will be forwarded on application.

Published annually, price 1s 6d., sewed, or 2s. 6d. cloth,

The Congregational Year Book. Containing

the Proceedings of the Congregational Union and General Statistics of the Denomination.

₊ The large circulation of the above, and its constant use as a work of reference, recommend it as a desirable medium for ADVERTISEMENTS, a scale of charges for which is subjoined :—

Six Lines and under	£0 8 0	A Whole Page	£2 10 0
Every Additional Line	0 1 0	Bills of Eight Pages and under	2 10 0
Half a Page	1 7 6	Not exceeding Sixteen Pages...	3 3 0

Advertisements should be sent to the Publishers by the 12th, and Bills (6000) by the 16th of December.

Congregational Church Records. A Series of

Papers prepared by the Committee of the Congregational Union, for recording Historical Facts relating to Churches, Minutes of Proceedings, &c., &c. Folio, bound in green vellum.

1st size, containing 2 quires, price 14s. | 2nd size, containing 4 quires, price 20s.
3rd size, containing 6 quires, price 26s.

The Contents and Proportions of the smallest sized book are as follows :—

Title Page, &c.	6 pages.	Roll of Church Members	32 pages.
Historical Account	12 ,,	Marriages	12 ,,
Church Minutes	96 ,,	Baptisms	24 ,,
Collections	12 ,,	Burials	12 ,,

The second size contains twice the above quantities ; and the third, three times.

Now ready, price One Shilling, cloth limp, red edges,

The Congregational Manual, containing Tracts

on Church Membership, Baptism, and the Lord's Supper, together with the Declaration of Faith, Church Order, and Discipline;

Or, separately, as below :

Congregational Tracts. Second Series.

No. 1—**Christian Baptism.** One Shilling and Sixpence per dozen.
No. 2—**The Lord's Supper**; its Design and Obligation. Two Shillings per doz.
No. 3—**A Guide to Church Membership.** Two Shillings per dozen.

ALSO,

The Declaration of Faith, Church Order, and Discipline. Price One Penny, or Five Shillings per hundred.

SCHOOL BOOKS.

Le Petit Precepteur ; or, First Steps to
French Conversation. By F. GRANDINEAU, formerly French
Master to Her Majesty Queen Victoria. Thirtieth Edition,
square 16mo., with Fifty Woodcuts, 3s. cloth.

Il Piccolo Precettore ; or, First Steps to
Italian Conversation. With Woodcuts, 3s. cloth.

Der Kleine Lehrer ; or, First Steps to German
Conversation. Uniform with "Le Petit Precepteur." 3s. cloth.

Select English Poetry. Designed for the use
of Schools and Young Persons in general. Edited by the late
Dr. ALLEN. Thirteenth Edition. Royal 18mo., price 4s. cloth.

Hymns for Infant Minds. By Ann and Jane
TAYLOR. 46th Edition. Price 1s. 6d. cloth.

By the same Authors,

Original Hymns for Sunday Schools. New
Edition. Price 2d. sewed.

First Lessons in Geography, in Question and
Answer. 220th Thousand. 18mo., sewed, 1s.

First Lessons in the Life of our Lord Jesus
Christ. For Families and Schools. By CHARLES WILLS, M.A.
18mo., cloth limp, 1s.

First Lessons in Astronomy, in Question and
Answer. Sixth Edition. 18mo., sewed, 1s.

First Lessons in the History of England, in
Question and Answer. On the plan of "First Lessons in
Geography." Sixteenth Edition. 18mo., sewed, 1s.

First Lessons on the Evidences of Christianity.
By B. B. WOODWARD, B.A., F.S A., Librarian to the Queen.
Second Edition. Cloth limp, 1s.

By the same Author,

First Lessons on the English Reformation.
Second Edition. Cloth limp, 1s..

WORKS FOR THE YOUNG.

A New One-Volume Edition of

The Child's Commentator on the Holy Scrip-

tures. By INGRAM COBBIN, M.A. Handsomely bound in em-
bossed cloth, gilt edges, with Twelve Coloured Engravings, and
Numerous Illustrations on Wood, price 7s. 6d.

"A most captivating volume."—*Evangelical Magazine.*
"This most excellent work."—*Sunday School Union Magazine.*
"The various texts are well illustrated, and the printing and binding are
superb."—*Public Opinion.*

SUNDAY SERVICES AT HOME.

Sabbath Teachings; or, the Children's Hour.

Being a Series of Short Services for Sundays at Home. By
BAILY GOWER. Elegantly bound in cloth, price 2s. 6d.

"It will admirably supply a want which has been long felt at home on the
Sabbath where children cannot go to the House of God to worship, and it will be a
source of as much interest to the young as it will be of gratification to their parents."
—*Wesleyan Times.*

The Teacher's Offering for 1864. Handsomely

bound in cloth, price 2s., Illustrated. The New Series complete,
Two Volumes in One, cloth gilt, price 3s. 6d. The Vol. for 1863
may still be had separately, price 2s., cloth gilt.

Sacred Harmonies for the Sabbath School and

Family. By JAMES SAMPSON. Price 1s., or 2s. roan, gilt edges.

"It comes much nearer to our own idea of what music for children ought to be
than anything we have met with before."—*Christian Spectator.*

The Bible Story-Book. By the Rev. B. H.

DRAPER. Thirteenth Edition, with Wood Engravings, price
2s. 6d., cloth gilt.

"Children of four and five read it with avidity, and never tire till the last story is
reached, and then they begin again. These 'Bible Stories' are worth a cart-load of
the Sunday-school novels of the day."—*Evangelical Magazine.*

Mary and her Mother: Scriptural Stories for

Young Children. Fifth Edition, 18mo., with Engravings and a
Frontispiece, 2s. 6d. cloth.

The Contributions of Q. Q. By Jane Taylor.

Twelfth Edition, with Vignette Title, in fcap. 8vo., price 5s. cloth,

THE MOTHERS' FRIEND.

A Magazine suitable for circulation among the Working Classes, to whom it is more particularly addressed. The attention of Tract Distrib..tors, City Missionaries, and Bible Women, is specially called to this periodical for gratuitous and loan purposes The Monthly circulation (price One Penny) has already reached 21,000.

The Volume for 1864, price 1s. 6d., cloth limp.

Volumes I. to IV., New Series, may also be had, price 1s. 6d. each.

FOR GENERAL CIRCULATION.

Principles to Start with : a Word to Young Men. By
Isaac Watts, D.D. With Preface by Rev. T. Binney. Price 4d., gilt edges.

Jesus Only. A Guide to the Anxious and a Companion
to the Sick Chamber and the Dying Bed. By the Rev. J. Oswald Jackson. Cheap Edition. Fourth Thousand, price 6d., limp covers.

"A plain practical exposition of the way of salvation."—*Sunday School Teacher's Magazine.*

The Easy Text-Book for Young People. By E. M. V.
Price 6d., cloth limp, red edges.

Secret Prayer. By Rev. C. Stanford, Author of "Central
Truths." Tenth Thousand, price 2s. per dozen.

By the same Author,

Friendship with God. Eighth Edition, price 2s. per doz.
Also, by the same Author,

The Presence of God our Rest. A New Year's Address.
Price 2s. per dozen.

Where shall I be 100 Years hence? By J. Metcalfe
White, B.A. Thirtieth Thousand, price 2s. per dozen.

By the same Author,

Sandy Foundations. 3s. per dozen.

Imputed Righteousness. By the Rev. Edward Steane,
D.D. Cheap Edition, price 1s. 6d. per dozen.

By the same Author,

The Great Transaction. Cheap Edition, 1s. 6d. per doz.
Also, by the same Author,

Prayer the Christian's Relief in Trouble. In 32mo.,
price 6d., cloth limp.

A Catechism of Christian Evidences, Truths, and Duties.
By the Rev. W. Walford, Author of "Curæ Romanæ," &c., &c. In 18mo., price 4d., or 3s. 6d. per dozen.

A Few Counsels to a Member of a Christian Church.
By the Rev. C. M. Birrell. Price 2s. per dozen.

By the same Author,

A Few Counsels to a Young Believer. Fifteenth Thousand,
Price 2s. per dozen.

Directions to Persons just commencing a Religious Life.
Second Edition, price 2s. per dozen.

www.ingramcontent.com/pod-product-compliance
Lightning Source LLC
Chambersburg PA
CBHW030550040726
47497CB00008B/2649